# Playing
# Beatie Bow

# Ruth Park

# Playing Beatie Bow

*Atheneum*          *New York*

Atheneum
Macmillan Publishing Company
866 Third Avenue, New York, NY 10022
Collier Macmillan Canada, Inc.

Printed in the United States of America

First Edition

5 7 9 11 13 14 15 17 19    20 18 16 14 12 10 8 6 4

LIBRARY OF CONGRESS CATALOGING IN PUBLICATION DATA

Park, Ruth.
Playing beatie bow.

An Argo Book
SUMMARY: A lonely Australian girl from a divided family
is transported back to the 1880s and an immigrant
family from the Orkney Islands.
[1. Family life—Fiction.   2. Space and time—Fiction.
3. Australia—Fiction]   I. Title.
PZ7.P2214Pl     [Fic]     81-8097
ISBN 0-689-30889-2     AACR2

# Playing
# Beatie Bow

# Chapter 1

In the first place, Abigail Kirk was not Abigail at all. She had been christened Lynette.

Her mother apologised. 'It must have been the anaesthetic. I felt as tight as a tick for days. And Daddy was so thrilled to have a daughter that he wouldn't have minded if I'd called you Ophelia.'

So for the first ten years of her life she was Lynnie Kirk, and happy as a lark. A hot-headed rag of a child, she vibrated with devotion for many things and people, including her parents. She loved her mother, but her father was a king.

So when he said good-bye to her, before he went off with another lady, she was outraged to the point of speechlessness that he could like someone so much better than herself that he didn't want to live in the same house with her any more.

'I'll come and see you often, Lynnie, I promise I shall,' he had said. And she, who could not bear to see a puppy slapped or a cockroach trodden on, hit him hard on the nose. She had never forgotten his shocked eyes above the blood-stained handkerchief. Very blue eyes they were, for he was half Norwegian.

Later she commanded her mother: 'Don't ever call me Lynnie again. Or any of those other names either.'

Kathy Kirk knew that her daughter was referring to

1

the many pet names her father called her, for she was very dear to him.

Because she was a loving woman, she had put her arms round the little girl and said, 'You don't understand, because you're too young yet. Just because Daddy wants to go away from me doesn't mean that he doesn't love you. But of course you may change your name if you wish. What would you like to be called?'

Weeks and months went past, and the person who had once been Lynette Kirk had no name at all. She would not answer to Lynette at home or at school. There were some puzzled notes from her teachers, which fortunately never had to be answered; because soon after the marriage break-up Kathy Kirk sold the family home and moved into a unit her husband had given her.

Her daughter was enraged that Kathy had accepted it. It was the finest in a high-rise tower her father's firm had designed, a glistening spike of steel and glass jammed in the sandstone amongst the tiny meek cottages and old bond stores of that part of Sydney called The Rocks.

'You ought to be prouder!' she yelled in her passion and grief. 'I'd rather live in the Ladies on the Quay than in something he gave me.'

'Be quiet!' said Grandmother in her razor-blade voice.

'You!' shouted that long-ago child. 'You're glad he's gone. *I* know.'

Because she was right, this was what began Abigail's and her grandmother's silent agreement not to like each other.

Yet, strangely, it was through Grandmother that the ex-Lynette at last found her name.

'You'll have to do something about that hysterical little bore, Katherine,' she said. Grandmother had this spooky habit of turning her eyes up and apparently speaking to a careful careless wave that curled down over her forehead. Lynnie always thought of it as Grandmother talking to her perm. Now she was doing it again. 'Just look at her, dear. She looks like a little witch with those wild eyes and her hair all in a bush.'

'You leave Lynnie alone, Mother! I've had enough of your sniping!' said Kathy in a voice in which Grandmother heard the fury and Lynette heard the shakiness.

'Well!' said Grandmother protestingly to her perm, for her daughter Kathy was a sunny-natured young woman and almost never lost her temper.

'Don't mind, darling,' said Kathy to ex-Lynette.

But the ex-Lynette was taken by the idea of being a witch.

'Tell me some witches' names, Mum,' she said.

'Well, there's Samantha, and Tabitha,' Kathy began.

'Oh, I don't want soppy TV names,' said her daughter. 'Some real witches' names.'

'They'd have to be old ones,' said Kathy thoughtfully, 'like Hephzibah, or Susannah, or Petronella, or Abigail.'

'That's the one!' cried the girl.

'But it's so plain, so knobbly, so . . . so awful!' wailed Kathy.

Grandmother smiled. Abigail could see quite easily that Grandmother thought she was plain and knobbly and awful, too. So that settled it.

'From now on I'm Abigail Kirk,' she said, 'and as soon as I'm old enough I'll change the Kirk, too.'

So time passed, one way and another. Now she was fourteen and, as with many other girls of her age, her inside did not match her outside at all. The outside was nothing to beat drums about. Somehow she had missed her mother's winning quaintness and her father's ash-blond distinction. She was thin and flat as a board, with a narrow

3

brown face and black coffee eyes so deep-set that she had only to cry for ten minutes and they disappeared altogether. This was one reason why she never cried.

She was known in the family as a clever student, a reserved girl, self-contained.

'More to that one than meets the eye,' said her grandmother with an ice-cream smile. 'Dodgy.'

Instead of tweaking off Grandmother's glasses and cracking them smartly across the edge of the table, as was her impulse, Abigail gave the old woman an ice-cream smile in return. Thereby proving that she was, perhaps, dodgy.

Or a girl who wished to be private.

Outside, she was composed, independent, not very much liked. The girls at school said she was a weirdie, and there was no doubt she was an outsider. She looked like a stick in jeans and a tank top; so she would not wear them. If everyone else was wearing her hair over her face, Abigail scraped hers back. She didn't have a boy friend, and when asked why she either looked enigmatic as though she knew twenty times more about boys than anyone else, or said she'd never met one who was half-way as interesting as her maths textbook. The girls said she was unreal, and she shrugged coolly. The really unreal thing was that she didn't care in the least what they thought of her. She felt a hundred years older and wiser than this love-mad rabble in her class.

Her chief concern was that no one, not even her mother, should know what she was like inside. Because maybe to adults the turmoil of uncertainties, extravagant glooms, and sudden blisses, might present some kind of pattern or map, so that they could say, 'Ah, so that's the real Abigail, is it?'

The thought of such trespass made her stomach turn

4

over. So she cultivated an expressionless face, a long piercing glance under her eyelashes that Grandmother called slippery. She carefully laid false trails until she herself sometimes could not find the way into her secret heart. Yet the older she grew the more she longed for someone to laugh at the false trails with, to share the secrets.

What secrets? She didn't yet know what they were herself.

The May holidays always made her feel forlorn and restless. Maybe it was the chill in the air after all the summer softness, the leaves turning yellow, letting go, whirling away. The dark coming earlier, as though the solitude of space were more tightly enclosing the earth, sunless and melancholy.

It was not possible to go for a holiday, unless it were to her grandmother's, which was unthinkable for them both. So, if her mother didn't want her to help at the shop, she spent hours squashed into the corner of the brown armchair, which had once been a kindly bear and now was only a bear-shaped chair near a window which looked out on cranes and mast tops, on the deck of the Harbour Bridge and the pearly cusps of the Opera House rising through the gauzy murk like Aladdin's palace.

Mumping, her mother called it. But she was not doing that, or even thinking. Mostly she was just aware of something missing.

When she was young she thought it was her father, for she had missed him miserably as well as hating him. Then with a new school and home, and new things to think about, she began to forget about him a little, though even now she could sometimes almost cry with pity for that woebegone, puzzled kid who used to go to bed and pray that her father would fall off a scaffold on one of his inspection tours, and the next moment sweat in terror in case he did.

But now she wasn't a kid she knew that it wasn't the absence of her father that caused the empty place inside. It was a part of her and she didn't know what it was or why it was there.

She and her mother, although they were such different characters, had fought and hugged and scrambled their way through to a close friendship. Kathy became a business-woman of flair and dash.

When the Kirk family lived in a two-car garden suburb, she had been a fearful packrat, a collector of almost everything. Abigail remembered wet days when big cardboard cartons and wooden tea-chests were thrown open to her and her playmates, and they had turned the entire house into a gorgeous mess of twinkles, spangles, seashells, face-less calico cats; old shoes; a real clown suit still stained with red and black grease-paint; Victorian postcards, some rude; and books and books of dried ferns, painted rosebuds, and autographs with silly poems.

After Abigail's father went away, Kathy had given a last decisive sniff, washed her face, which was somewhat like that of a fat-cheeked finch with a finch's shiny dew-drop eyes, raked her hair up on top of her head in a washerwoman's knot, and rented a black hole of Calcutta in a Paddington lane. This she turned into a treasure-house of trendy trivia. She called the shop Magpies, and soon other magpie people flocked around to shriek and snatch and buy.

What with Kathy being a success, and Grandmother getting more interested in Bridge and less of a carper, Abigail and her mother achieved a kind of happiness.

Now she jumped up with a scowl, banged the door on the empty place, and went to visit the Crowns, her neighbours.

That unit was in its customary state of theatrically awful mess. Justine Crown didn't believe in housework. She said the children came first; but she hadn't made a gold-medal job of them either. Usually Natalie, the four-year-old, was at kindergarten, and Vincent, the high-rise monster, at school. But as it was holidays they were both at home, and Vincent, who was in Abigail's opinion the grimmest kid two agreeable people could be cursed with, was at his usual game of worrying Natalie like a dog with a bone.

Natalie aroused in Abigail a solemnly protective feeling. This rather embarrassed her. The little girl was prone to sudden fevers, nightmares, fears, and had a kind of helpless affection for the frightful Vincent that did not allow her to defend herself against him.

Vincent was a bundle of bones with a puzzling smell, as though he'd wet himself six weeks earlier and not bothered to bathe. He was as sharp as a knife and had his parents sized up to the last millimetre. Abigail did not see that his face was wretched as well as cunning, and she was sincerely flattered that he hated her more than he hated everyone else.

'You've got Dracula teeth,' he greeted her.

Justine shouted from the kitchen, 'Oh, for heaven's sake don't start on Abigail, you little beast.' She came out, bashing around in a basin with a fork. 'He's been dark blue hell all day.'

'Dracula teeth,' said Vincent. 'Big long white choppers. See them, Fat Nat?'

'Don't call your sister that, and if Abigail's teeth are too big it's because her face hasn't grown up to them yet.'

Instantly Abigail imagined herself with this thin nosy face and fangs sticking out over her lower lip.

She was very depressed with her looks as it was, and had given up hope of developing fascinating high cheekbones or eyelashes an inch long. She liked her eyebrows, which were black and straight, and her long brown hair, which glistened satisfactorily. But although her mother assured her that her figure would arrive some day, she often despaired. Most times people took her for twelve, which was humiliating.

However, she was not going to be bugged by any six-year-old dinosaur like Vincent Crown. She glared at him.

'Knock off the wisecracks!' To Justine she said, 'It's freezing outside, but would you like me to take them down to the playground till it starts to get dark?'

Justine was so jubilant at the thought of being free of Natalie's unexplained tears and silences and Vincent's whining that she had the children into their anoraks and woolly caps before Abigail could think, 'Curse it, why am I such a sucker?'

The high-rise tower was called Mitchell, after a famous man who had been born just where it stood many years before. He was the Mitchell who founded the Mitchell Library. High-rise buildings near by were called Dalley, Campbell, and Reiby, after other celebrated people, though Abigail didn't know for what they were celebrated.

Mitchell stood amongst charming landscaping, which included a covered swimming-pool and a children's playground. In spite of her resentment against her father, Abigail could never hate the building, standing up there severe as a sword, slitting each wind into two streams, reflecting fish-scale seas, and cherry-red sunsets, and a city which, when stretched and crinkled by curved windows, grew itself steeples and domes and trees like minarets, and escarpments floating in cloud. On the lobby wall in polished brass were the letters: *Architects: Weyland Kirk, Casper and Domenici, Sydney, San Francisco, Oslo, Siena.* Abigail tried never to look at it, for, try as she might, she couldn't help feeling proud: she knew that this particular high-riser was all the work of Weyland Kirk.

Now Mitchell was haughtily slicing up a barbed westerly, which did not seem to bother the children climbing the monkey bars, brawling thunderously inside the concrete pipes, or fighting like tom-cats inside the space rocket. Thankfully Abigail released Vincent's hard, sticky paw, and he flitted off to torment a group of fat bundles climbing the stone wall about the playground. Let the fat bundles look after themselves, Abigail thought callously. Likely they'd have parents with them, anyway, who would pluck Vincent away from their darlings and, with any luck, half-strangle him in the process.

The noise was shattering. Most of the children came from Mitchell, but others probably lived in the cottages round about. Abigail observed that those racing dementedly back and forth performed their charges in a certain order. They were playing a group game.

'Would you like to play it, too, Natty?'

Natalie shook her head. Her big grey eyes were now full of tears. Abigail sighed. Justine was for ever trailing Natalie off to a doctor who was supposed to be miraculous with highly strung children, but he hadn't brought off any miracles yet.

'Now what's the matter, little dopey?'

'They're playing Beatie Bow and it scares me. But I like to watch. Please let's watch,' pleaded Natalie.

'Never heard of it,' said Abigail. She noticed Vincent rushing to join in and thought how weird it was that in the few years that had passed since she was six or seven the kids had begun to play such different games. She watched this one just in case Vincent murdered anyone. She could already hear him squealing like a mad rat.

Natalie took hold of a fistful of her shawl, and Abigail held her close to keep her out of the wind. The child was shivering. Yet the game didn't look so exciting; just one more goofy kid's game.

9

First of all the children formed a circle. They had become very quiet. In the middle was a girl who had been
chosen by some counting-out rhyme.

'That's Mudda,' explained Natalie.

'What's Mudda?'

'You know, a mummy like my mummy.'

'Oh, Mother!'

'Yes, but she's called Mudda. That's in the game.'

Someone hidden behind the concrete pipes made a
scraping sound. The children chorused, 'Oh, Mudda,
what's that?'

'Nothing at all,' chanted the girl in the centre. 'The dog
at the door, the dog at the door.'

Now a bloodcurdling moan was heard from behind the
pipes. Abigail felt Natalie press closer to her. She noticed
that the dark was coming down fast; soon it would rain.
She resolved she would take the children home as soon as
she could gather up Vincent.

'Oh, Mudda, what's that, what can it be?'

'The wind in the chimney, that's all, that's all.'

There was a clatter of stones being dropped. Some of the
younger children squawked, and were hushed.

'Oh, Mudda, what's that, what's that, can you see?'

'It's the cow in the byre, the horse in the stall.'

Natalie held on tightly and put her hands over her eyes.

'Don't look, Abigail, it's worse than awful things on
TV!'

At this point Mudda pointed dramatically beyond the
circle of children. A girl covered in a white sheet or tablecloth was creeping towards them, waving her arms and
wailing.

'It's Beatie Bow,' shrieked Mudda in a voice of horror,
'risen from the dead!'

At this the circle broke and the children ran shrieking

10

hysterically to fling themselves in a chaotic huddle of arms and legs in the sandpit at the other end.

'What on earth was all that about?' asked Abigail. She felt cold and grumpy and made gestures at Vince to rejoin them.

'The person who is Beatie Bow is a ghost, you see,' explained Natalie, 'and she rises from her grave, and everyone runs and pretends to be afraid. If she catches someone, that one has to be the next Beatie Bow. But mostly the children *are* frightened, because they play it and play it till it's dark. Vincent gets in a state and that's why he's so mean afterwards. But the little furry girl doesn't get scared,' she added inconsequentially. 'I think she'd like to join in, she smiles so much. Look, Abigail, see her watching over there?'

Before the older girl could look, Vincent panted up, scowling.

'We're going to play it again! I want to! I want to!'

'No way,' said Abigail firmly. 'It's getting dark and it's too cold for Natalie already.'

The boy said bitterly, 'I hate you!'

'Big deal,' said Abigail.

Vincent pinched Natalie cruelly. Tears filled her eyes. 'You see? Just like I told you,' she said without rancour.

'What a creep you are, Vincent,' said Abigail scornfully.

Vincent made a rude gesture and ran on before them into the lobby. As they waited for the lift, Abigail saw that his whole body was trembling. She made up her mind to have a word with Justine about the too-exciting game.

'I saw the little furry girl, Vince,' said Natalie. 'She was watching you all again.'

He ignored her, barged past them into the Crown unit, and flung himself down before the TV.

'I'll stay a little while if you like, Justine,' offered Abigail.

'Mum won't be home till nearly seven. She had to go and look at some old furniture at St Mary's near Penrith.'

Justine was delighted at the prospect of concluding dinner preparations without the usual civil war between her young. She suggested that Abigail help Natty make new clothes for her teddy-bear.

Abigail enjoyed sewing, and made some of her own clothes. She did not do a professional job, but she did her best; and somehow she loved her clothes more because of the sleeves that wouldn't quite fit, the seams she had unpicked over and over again. At the moment she was fond of long dresses and shawls and hooded sweaters. Her favourite belt was a piece of old harness strap, polished deep brown and fastened with the original brass buckles. It had a phantom smell of horse which her grandmother said was disgusting.

'You look like a gipsy or a street Arab,' she said.

'The Arabs own all the streets nowadays, Grandmother.' Abigail smiled. 'You're not up with things.'

'Don't be impertinent!' snapped Grandmother. She appealed to her perm. 'Katherine, are you going to stand there and permit this child to speak to me like that?'

'You criticised her clothes, Mother,' answered Kathy, flushing. 'She didn't say a word about yours.'

'About mine?' gasped Grandmother, as though it had never occurred to her that she was not wearing the only type of garment in the world. She swept out – she really did sweep in some extraordinary way – and Kathy looked rueful and fidgety, for she hated to be at outs with anyone.

'All right, don't be sarky,' she said to her daughter. 'You can dress any way you like. But please try not to aggravate her deliberately. She's old and . . .'

'Oh, Mum,' said Abigail impatiently, 'she enjoys a little

12

set-to. It improves her circulation or something. That's why she always used to pick on Dad. Don't you remember how her eyes used to sparkle . . .' She stopped dead. Why had she brought Dad into it? She sneaked a sidelong glance at her mother, and saw that Kathy's eyes were full of tears.

'I was pretty dumb in those days,' said Kathy. Then she laughed, and began to peel vegetables for dinner. But she was still flushed.

Now as they rummaged in the ragbag, trying that piece and this against Teddy's stubby form, Abigail told the little girl that she had almost finished making herself a long dress from an Edwardian curtain that her mother had found in a box of old fabrics bought at an auction. The curtain was still unperished, a heavy cotton with strong striped selvages, which Abigail had wangled around to use as borders for sleeves and skirt.

'It's a very funny colour,' she told Natalie. 'A mucky brownish-green, like pea soup.'

'It wouldn't suit Teddy,' observed Natalie.

'And Teddy is not going to get it either,' said Abigail.

They cut out a pair of red shorts, and Abigail tacked them up for Justine to sew. Then they upended the ragbag to find something spotted for a waistcoat. Tangled amongst all the scraps and remnants and outgrown garments was a strangely shaped piece of yellowed crochet. Abigail smoothed it out, trying to distinguish the pattern. It was very fine work, almost like lace.

Justine came in, battled with Vincent about his bath before dinner, and dragged him away. She came back.

'What have you got there? Oh, that old rag! It's been around for ever. Give it to me, Abigail, and I'll use it for a dishcloth or something.'

13

'If you don't want it,' said the girl, 'I'd really like to have it.'

She spread the crumpled fabric. 'See, it's a yoke for a high-necked dress. Just right for my new greeny one.'

'It's yours,' said Justine cheerfully. 'Probably fall to bits the first time you wash it.'

The children were quiet and, since Mr Crown was due home, Abigail said good-bye and went. She was very taken with Justine's gift. She decided against bleaching the crochet piece, for the chemical might be too harsh for the old thread. Besides, she liked the creamy colour against the murky green of the dress. She carefully washed the yoke and dried it with a hair-dryer, stretching the fabric as she went. The pattern showed itself at last as a recurrent design of a delicate plant with a flower like a buttercup rising out of five heart-shaped leaves.

With a cry of pleasure, Abigail saw that each flower had been over-embroidered with yellowish green tiny knots which seemed to indicate stamens or hairs. But the coloured thread had so faded that it was almost indiscernible.

About seven, her mother telephoned. She sounded tired, said she had been delayed, and told Abigail to go ahead and eat something. The girl agreed and went back to her work.

The border of the crochet was a curious twist, almost like a rope, done in a coarser thread, and at the edge of each shoulder Abigail saw, between the leaves of a flower, the tiny initials A.T.

As she worked, she found herself singing, 'The cow in the byre, the horse in the stall.' She broke off. 'Now where did those kids hear a funny word like byre?'

By the time Kathy had tottered in and collapsed in a chair, Abigail already had the crochet tacked to the dress. Weary as she was, her mother exclaimed at it.

14

'It's a Victorian piece, I think, although the pattern is unfamiliar. What superb work! I could sell it like a shot if you want me to.'

'No,' said Abigail.

'Don't blame you. Heavens, I'm bushed. No, I don't want anything to eat. Had a bite in town. Sorry, love. Have to fall into bed.'

She limped off, yawning like a lion. Abigail stitched the yoke to her dress with the smallest stitches she could achieve: the fineness of her new treasure seemed to demand it. The yoke fitted the bodice as though it had been made for it, and when she tried on the dress it was as if the two pieces of fabric had never been separate. The girl had an extraordinary sense of pleasure. She felt that she would wear this perfect dress until it fell to bits. Even now she knew that this was one of those mysterious garments in which she always felt happy.

Just before she went to sleep she thought, 'I've seen that flower somewhere. Not real though. A picture.'

At the same moment she recalled the old *Herbal* in the bookcase. She squeezed her eyes tight and tried to go to sleep, but it was no use. She had to get out of bed and look. She riffled through the thick fox-marked pages to the wild-flowers, and there it was: not a buttercup at all, but a peat bog plant called Grass of Parnassus.

Parnassus! Was the plant Greek then? She knew that Parnassus was where the Muses lived, the goddesses of poetry and dance and art and whatever the rest of them were. Parnassus was a lovely word, and perhaps the original Parnassus had grass that was not ordinary grass but blossomed with little hairy flowers of green and faded yellow.

Suddenly she felt intensely happy, almost as blissfully happy as she had been before she was ten, knowing nothing

15

of the world but warmth and sunshine, and loving parents and birthdays and Christmas presents.

She floated off to sleep. She did not dream of an enchanted mountain where goddesses danced and sang, but of a smell of burning sugar, and a closed door with an iron fist for a knocker, and tied to the fist a bit of yellow rag.

# Chapter 2

At breakfast next morning her mother was fully recovered, talkative and bright-cheeked. She admired the new dress, puzzled over the crochet pattern, and voted for Agnes Timms as the owner of the initials A.T. But Abigail said that, since the design seemed to be of a Greek plant, A.T. probably stood for Anastasia Tassiopolis, or something similar.

Kathy chattered on until at last her daughter said teasingly, 'What are you excited about, Apple Annie? Did you find something extra special at St Mary's?'

Kathy's eyes twinkled. 'I might as well tell you. I had dinner with your father last night.'

Weyland Kirk and his wife had never been divorced. Their relations were friendly, and two or three times a year they met to discuss business matters or Abigail's future. Abigail was occasionally taken out by her father to some entertainment; and although they both behaved with careful courtesy it was always an awkward and hateful experience for Abigail. Something lay between them, an ineradicable memory of rejection of love, and Abigail could not pretend it was not there.

He asked her polite questions about her friends, even the ones he could remember from her childhood and she had almost forgotten.

'You seem to be a bit of a loner, pet,' he said, almost apologetically.

She answered coolly, 'I really don't care for people much.'

He had the same quickness of uptake as she, and he shot her a blue glance that laid her thoughts bare. Then he said gently, 'Well, you can always trust your mother, anyway.'

She knew how much she had hurt him. She tried to be glad. He deserved it. But she was not glad; she was sorry and ashamed.

Now she looked without concern at her mother and said 'Oh, yes? Did you just run into him?'

'As a matter of fact I've seen him quite a few times lately,' Kathy said. 'Oh, darling, don't be cross. I know it was deceitful of me, but I thought I wouldn't mention it in case it all fell through.'

Abigail felt a sudden chill. 'Whatever are you talking about, Mum?'

'Oh, Abigail, I don't know how to put it without sounding silly. Dad – well, he wants us to become a family again.'

'You're joking,' said Abigail.

Kathy's face was almost pleading. 'No, I'm not.'

Abigail felt much as she had felt that morning her father had said good-bye. A burning wave of dismay, anger and fright swept up from her feet. But before it reached her face and turned it scarlet she managed to say, 'And what about Miss Thingo? Is she going to join the party?'

Kathy said stiffly, 'You know very well Jan went off to Canada a year ago. She has a name. Use it, and don't be vulgar. What do you think I'm talking about, last Saturday's TV movie? This is a serious matter for me and your father, so please don't fool about with it.'

Abigail could hardly believe what she heard. 'You're really considering it! After what he did four years ago?'

18

Kathy smiled nervously. She used a cool tone, but it did not go well with her restless hands. 'Next thing you'll be saying he tossed me aside like a worn-out glove.'

'He dumped you and me for a scheming little creep on his secretarial staff, that's what he did, after being married twelve years.'

'Hold on,' said Kathy. 'Fair's fair. Jan wasn't like that at all. And besides that, he fell in love with her. You don't even know what that means yet.'

'Oh, Mum, now you're being wet!'

'Oh, I know all you schoolgirls think you know every last word in the book about the relationships between a man and a woman; but love is a thing you have to experience before you know –' she hesitated, and then blurted out – 'how powerful it can be.'

'Oh, come on!'

'I'm only thirty-six,' said Kathy. 'I've missed being married.'

Abigail leapt up and began to pile the dishes noisily in the sink.

'You've no self-respect!'

'Okay, okay!' cried Kathy. 'It's awful, it's shameful, it isn't liberated in the slightest – but I happen to love Weyland. I always have, and I always wanted him to come back. And now it's happened and I want to go with him.'

Abigail was so outraged, so disgusted that anyone as capable and independent and courageous as her mother could be so . . . so – *female* was the word that sprang to her mind – that for a moment the significance of what she had said did not strike her.

'What do you mean, *go?*' she said, aghast.

'He has to go to Norway for three years of architectural study, and he wants us to go with him and . . . and be together again as we used to.'

Abigail felt as if her mother had risen and hit her with the teapot. 'Norway! Why Norway?'

'Well, he's always had this strong feeling for Scandinavian design, because of his family, I expect. But he wouldn't be in Norway all the time. He has to take some seminars in the University of Oslo, and of course we could often go to Denmark . . . and England sometimes.' Her voice trailed away.

'Mother,' said Abigail, 'don't you realise that he could easily leave you again?'

'Yes,' admitted Kathy. 'I have to take the risk, you see.'

Flushing, she looked at her daughter, and the innocence and frankness of that gaze was such that Abigail thought, amazed, 'She really *is* in love with him; she has been all along.'

Such jealousy fired up in her heart that she felt dizzy.

'Then you can take it by yourself.'

Her mother looked as if she had been slapped. 'You can't mean that, darling.'

'You forget that he dumped me, too,' said Abigail tartly. 'That's not going to happen to me again. I can't stop you doing something idiotic if that's what you want, but you can't make me do it, too.'

'But, Abigail, how can I . . . I can't leave you here at your age!'

The shock of realisation hit Abigail. 'She'd really leave me, if there had to be a choice.'

Pride forced the hurt into the back of her mind. With an effort she composed her face. She even smiled.

'Oh, well, let's be practical, Mum. I can easily change over to boarding-school until I'm ready for university, and then I'll go and flat with someone, or live in college.'

'Oh, no!'

'Don't try to wheedle me out of it, Mum. I'm not going. No way.'

Her exit was spoiled because the door slipped out of her fingers and slammed. She couldn't very well open it again and explain to her mother that she wasn't so childish as to go around slamming doors. She stood in the middle of her bedroom feeling sick with fury and shock and a horrible kind of triumph, because she knew how much she had wounded her mother.

'She's hurt because she knows I'm right. How could she, how could she be like that, with all she's got – me, and the shop, and her friends and . . . ?' Here a burst of anger made her feel sickish. 'And Dad! The nerve of . . .'

Her mother tapped on the door. 'Abigail, I'd like you to come and help me unpack and catalogue some things today. I got so many items from St Mary's.'

'Thanks, but I don't want to,' answered Abigail curtly.

'But,' wailed Kathy, 'if you go to boarding-school where will you spend the holidays? You'd loathe it with Grandmother and we haven't anyone else. Oh, please, darling, I know it's been a surprise. I suppose I told you all the wrong way. But please come with me and let's talk it out down at Magpies.'

Abigail did not reply. After a while her mother gave the door a ferocious kick. The girl could not help grinning; Kathy was such a child.

After her mother had gone she washed up, and put on her green dress, which made her feel better. But not much better.

She had a terrible feeling that her mother would go to Norway, regardless. She could not mistake that look on her face. It was happiness and hope. All these years, then, she had longed and hankered for Weyland Kirk to come back to where she felt he belonged. It was like some late-late-show movie – brave little wife making the best of desertion and loneliness, and then one rainy night, gaunt and pale, in comes Gene Kelly. Oh, Kathy, can you ever forgive me? I made such a mistake. I ruined my life, but oh, how can I forgive myself for ruining yours? It's always been you, Kathy, always.

Bring up the reunited lovers music, and she falls into his arms and a bit later he dances up and down the stairs on his knees.

Abigail could just imagine what the girls at school would say. Some, the sloppy romantic ones, would think it just lovely. Together again! But the others, the toughies, would think it disgusting. Love was for the young, everyone knew that. Like having no wrinkles or varicose veins. And besides, they'd say her mother was being grovelly. He whistles and back she goes like a well-trained dog.

The more she thought about it the angrier and more embarrassed she felt. 'There's the shop, too. After all her hard work building it up. She's not thinking straight – early menopause or something. And what about me? Turning my life upside down once more for him? A lot he cared about me when I was little and needed him! I don't owe him anything,' thought Abigail, white with fury. 'Not one kind word.'

But, oh God, there was Grandmother, chic and glittery and poisonous and probably thrilled to her long claw toes to get her hands on a lonely Abigail and teach her what's what and who's who. Grandmother's house, expensive suburbia, with a surly houseman, Uruguayan or something, who lived in separate quarters at the end of the garden, the Bridge ladies, the theatre parties, and Abigail required to hand round the teensy bits of fish goo on decarbohydrated crackers. They were always on diets, the Bridge ladies, though not one of them had a soul in the world to care a spit if she turned into a porker or not.

She went around the unit saying, 'Norway!' She saw it as a kind of iceberg with houses on it. And Lapps, weren't there Lapps, with funny knitted hats with tops like two horns? Penguins? Polar bears, then. Norway, a million kilometres away from Sydney and the life she and Mum had made for themselves without Dad's help.

Alternatively she raged and sulked, and then reassured herself with little bursts of optimism. 'Of course she didn't mean it, that crazy lady. She'll think it over and see it doesn't make sense.'

And then she imagined Dad dancing up and down the stairs instead of Gene Kelly; but instead of laughing she cried, because even though she hated what he had done all those years ago she knew she still loved him and was afraid that if they lived together she'd come to love him still more and so could be hurt worse.

In this way the day went past dreadfully and speedily, and when the Bridge began to bellow with the home-going traffic she stirred herself, washed her face and, taking her shawl, she went next door.

'I'm bored, Justine. Like me to take the kids to the playground for a while?'

The young woman, who usually looked like a starved cat, now looked like a sleepless starved cat. She seemed at the end of her tether.

'If you could just take Natty off my hands. Goodness, how super! Vincent has been moaning all day, and I've just pried open his trap to look at his throat, and it's like a beetroot. I was just about to hustle him and Natalie along to the doctor. But if you could look after Nat –' She threw her arms thankfully about the girl. 'You're a pet, Abigail, bless you. Good heavens, is that the family tatting you have on your dress? I can't believe it.'

'Abigail has big Dracula teeth dripping with blood,' croaked Vincent.

'Oh, shut up, you,' she snapped. Justine looked pained

23

and Abigail felt ashamed, for after all the little viper *was* sick. She busied herself putting Natalie into her outdoor gear.

The child whispered excitedly, 'When I was watching through the window I saw the little furry girl.'

Abigail hugged her. 'You and your little furry girl! And how could you see her all the way down there in the playground?'

'I don't know; I just did. I wonder where she comes from?'

'I expect she lives in one of the little terrace houses,' said Abigail as they went down in the lift.

'I'd like to live in a little house,' said Natalie, 'with sunflowers higher than the roof and little hollows in the stairs. And a bedroom with a slopey roof. And a chimney.'

The little girl, freed from the oppressive presence of her brother, skipped blithely along, looking at the children sliding down slippery-dips, hanging on the bars like rows of orangoutangs and climbing over the gaudily painted locomotive that stood near the sandpit. Abigail lifted Natalie up to the driver's seat, but she was frightened at the height; and, besides, most of the children had begun their obsessive game of Beatie Bow, and she wanted to watch.

'Why do you want to watch when the silly game scares you so, Natty?'

'I just want to look at the little furry girl watching, because I like her, you see.'

'You're a funny little sausage.' Abigail sat on a cement mushroom and watched curiously while the children formed themselves into their hushed circle, and 'Mudda' took her place in the middle. Natalie pulled at her shawl.

'There she is, Abigail. Do look.'

Abigail looked. At the edge of the playground, absorbed in the children's activities, yet seemingly too shy to emerge from the half-shadow of the wall, was a diminutive figure in a dark dress and lighter pinafore. Her face was pale, and her hair had been clipped so close it did indeed look like a cat's fur. Eagerly she watched the children, smiling sometimes, or looking suspenseful, as the game went on, and then jumping up and down excitedly as Beatie Bow emerged from her grave and frightened everyone to death.

'I wonder why she doesn't play. Perhaps she's crippled or something,' said Abigail. 'Let's go and talk to her.'

They were close to the child before she noticed them, so engrossed was she. She was about eleven, Abigail thought, but stunted, with a monkey face and wide-apart eyes that added to the monkey look. She wore a long, washed-out print dress, a pinafore of brown cotton, and over both of them a shawl crossed over her chest and tied behind. Her feet were bare, and Abigail was surprised to see that the skin was peeling from them in big flakes.

'Hullo, little girl!' said Natty shyly.

The child whipped around in what seemed consternation. She looked an ugly, lively little creature, but scared to death. With a stifled squawk she fled along the wall and dived up one of the steep stone alleys that still linked the many irregular levels of The Rocks.

'Well, she didn't like *us*,' said Abigail. 'Or perhaps she comes from another country and didn't understand we wanted to be friends.'

Natalie nodded, her eyes full of tears once more.

'Oh, Natty, do stop crying. You're like a leaky jug or something. What's the matter now?'

'I don't know.' But when Abigail had delivered her back at the unit, she gave the elder girl a hug and whispered, 'I cried because the little furry girl has been unhappy.'

'How do you know?' Abigail asked, but the child just shook her head.

25

Kathy came home early. She had been steeling herself all day to face discussion of the problem of leaving Sydney.

'Now, Abigail, let's be straightforward and honest . . .'

'I am,' said Abigail. 'But before we get on to that, what are you going to do with Magpies?'

'Lucille said she'd buy it.'

'Wouldn't it be more sensible to lease it to her, so that you can get it back afterwards?'

'Afterwards!' gasped Kathy. 'Of all the cynical . . .' She had turned quite pale. 'If you want to know, Dad said he's never stopped caring for me.'

'And now for the violins,' said Abigail. The moment the words were out of her mouth she felt terrible, as if she'd taken up the vegetable knife and stuck it into her mother. As for Kathy, she exploded: 'That's a lousy thing to say. Especially from you. When did you ever feel anything for me when Dad left home? You were so wrapped up in your own troubles anyone might have thought no one else was hurt.'

'Well, you might remember I was only ten,' protested Abigail, aghast at this broadside from her mother who had never attacked her before.

'You've been twelve since then, and thirteen and fourteen, the wideawake kid who knows all about men and women and sex and love; and never, not once, have you ever said or asked anything about what I felt when Dad left. Did you ever think of me as a deserted wife, or just of yourself as a deserted child?' shouted Kathy. 'And now I have a chance to experience happiness again, you're going to throw a spanner in the works, because you know very well I won't leave you here with no one but Grandmother to look to if you get ill or . . . or . . . anything.'

She hurried off to the bathroom and spent so long there that Abigail went unhappily to bed.

26

The next morning Kathy said, 'If you're going to help at Magpies today we'd better get going. Are you?'

'Why not?' said Abigail, and she was glad to hear a voice that was hard and flip, as she wanted it to be.

And for the rest of the painful day, and all the next, no word passed between them except those of ordinary civility. Abigail was glad they were busy, for crates of stuff arrived from the old farm at St Mary's – oil paintings black with smoke and grease, battered colonial furniture, goldfish bowls and petit-point evening bags, and all the fascinating detritus of some unknown person's expended life.

Kathy looked as if she had been crying in the night, for she had put on eyeshadow, which she rarely did. She looked ridiculous, like a finch that had lost a fight. Abigail was so upset she felt dislocated; her emotions were so turbulent that she felt like some sea creature with horny shell and poisonous spines, and bits of weed and shell attached as camouflage. Except that all the camouflage she had was her cool expressionless face, and her green dress, which she kept stroking and touching, as though it gave her comfort, the way Natalie stroked her teddy-bear. And she went on doing this, unconsciously, until at last Kathy screamed:

'Stop that! You've been doing it all day; you're driving me up the wall. I wish you'd take that wretched dress off; it's too cold for this weather. Why do you get so obsessed with some stupid garment? It just sends me round the bend.'

'Maybe there's s-something else you'd like to find wrong with me while you're at it!' Abigail could not keep her voice from shaking. It was unreal. She and her mother did not go on like this. They were friends.

'Oh, shut up!' yelped Kathy, turning to her work.

Abigail grabbed her old patchwork shawl (it, too, had come from some deceased estate) and tore up to the corner of the street and caught a West Circular Quay bus. She sat there and boiled while the bus bumped and halted and jerked onwards, and inside the tears ran down and put out the fire of her anger.

It was true. She did wear things until they almost fell off. But always before her mother had laughed.

'That's Abigail, always rapt in something. And why not?' she had said. Already there was a change in both of them.

'It's true,' she thought, sorrowfully, 'I never did think of what she must have felt. Never once did I put my arms around her and say, "Don't mind, I'm still here." It was always Mum who did that to me.'

A bus seemed an unlikely place to have your heart broken in, but she felt that was happening. She didn't even have dark glasses to hide behind. All she could do was to open her burning eyes to their utmost so that the tears wouldn't fall out, and put on the calm, slightly scornful face she had, thank God, practised for years.

'It's all his fault, trying to creep in, spoiling what we have,' she thought. But it was not her father that her thoughts returned to over and over again, it was Mum. 'If she's loved him all this while, and not thought of anyone else, it must have been hell for her. But she's never complained, and when I made those snide remarks about Jan she even said I was unfair. I don't think I could ever say a good word for someone my husband left me for. But it's true, I would expect my only daughter to stand by me. And I didn't. I just thought of how awful it was for me, the way I'm doing right now.'

She had left the bus almost without noticing it. Great steely skies, blanched with approaching winter, arched overhead, and amidst these floated the half-circle of the

Bridge, spangled with crimson patches from the sunset, long gone but still painted on the high clouds. The windows of Mitchell and other tall buildings shone tremulously with this ruby light. A cold dusty wind blew from the south, bringing in gusts the iron voice of the city, the dirty, down-at-heel city around Central Railway, drowning the hoot of the hydrofoils, the swish-swash of ferries drawing in and pulling out at Circular Quay.

There were still children tearing around in the playground, and she halted for a moment to watch them. Mothers and older brothers were calling them in. There were not enough to play Beatie Bow; they were chasing each other, screeching aimlessly.

Her eyes turned instinctively to the corner of the wall where it met the street. There lurked Natalie's little furry girl, looking cold and forlorn.

'She looks the way I feel,' thought Abigail.

But how did she feel? Not quite lost but almost. Baffled. A sense of too many strange ideas crowding around her, a feeling of helplessness and difficulty with which she could not come to terms. She thought, 'Maybe they're right. Maybe there is such a thing as being too young and inexperienced to know your own mind.'

Or perhaps it was something simpler. In Norway, if there was family discord once more, she would have no bolt-holes, no familiar places or friends, probably not even anyone to whom she could speak in English. At the thought of this her sensation of vulnerability grew so strong that she almost cried out aloud.

'Mum's got to listen to me,' she thought. 'Maybe she could cope if something went wrong, but I couldn't, I know I couldn't.'

Distinctly she saw the little furry girl sigh, as though sadly disappointed.

And for an instant she reminded Abigail of Natalie,

when tormented beyond endurance by the demonic Vincent.

'Poor little rat,' she thought. 'The things kids have to put up with!'

All at once she had an irresistible desire to speak once more to this child, to find out why she watched, why her clothes were so poor, why Natalie thought she had been unhappy. Most of all she wanted to see her smile. She tiptoed along in the shadow of the wall. The little furry girl, looking hopefully at the children, did not see her.

'Boo!' whispered Abigail.

The child leapt in the air like a trout, gaping at Abigail. Her eyes were a light hazel, and Abigail noticed that her hair was tufted and bristly as though growing out after having been shaved.

'Did I give you a start?' she said. 'It was only a joke.'

The other blurted, 'I wasna doing naething! I were only watching the bairns!'

Her voice was hoarse, her accent so extraordinary that Abigail caught only a word or two. But before she could ask the girl to repeat what she had said, the hazel eyes glistened and she said in a half-sob, half-cough, 'I dunna want it to be true, but then again I do, oh, I do!'

This time Abigail heard clearly. Involuntarily she stretched out a hand to this odd troubled child as she might have done to Natty, but the girl leapt away like a hare up the cobbled lane she had used the previous time.

More for curiosity than anything else, Abigail stretched her long legs and raced up the steep alley.

She could not remember ever walking up it before, though it was directly opposite the playground. It ascended as abruptly as a staircase between tall stone walls of warehouses or shops. She did not have time to look. At the top was a little flight of crooked stone steps, and there she could see the child's shawl fluttering, as she hesitated and peered back at her pursuer. The shawl showed dark bottle-green under a street lamp.

'Don't be a silly little twit. I only want to talk to you,' cried Abigail breathlessly. She bounded up the steps into the light and saw that she was in Harrington Street, a queer old road, not much used now, all different levels, so that sometimes one had to step down from the footpath and other times up. The little girl had flickered out of the light, but Abigail could see her bare feet and the edge of her skirt showing in the shadow of a thickety shrub that had followed its network of snaky roots down the crevices of a crumbling stone embankment.

She called out teasingly, 'I can see you hiding there!'

Just then, down in the city, the Town Hall clock began its baritone booming, distorted and half drowned by the traffic. But Abigail distinctly heard the first four notes of the simple tune which denoted the half-hour, and she thought, 'Five thirty. I'd best be getting home, I suppose.'

Something, she did not know what, made her hold out her hand to the hidden child and say, in a doomed, dramatic voice. 'Oh, Mudda, what's that, what can it be?'

There was a muffled squeal of surprise or terror, Abigail could not guess which, from the little girl; but before she could make another move she heard a clinking and creaking and rattling and the unmistakable sound of a horse's hoofs. And out of the gathering dusk at the south end of Harrington Street, its two side-lamps shining dimly, for they held only stumps of candles, came a high old-fashioned cab, glittering black in the wavering light from the street lamp.

Abigail was stunned. She stood in the middle of the street, as though she'd lost all power to move, until she could see the very breath from the horse's nostrils in the cold air, and the panic on the face of the tall-hatted cabbie. His lips were curled back, displaying a black gap

31

in the middle of his teeth. He half rose.

'Get outa the road, wench! D'ye want to be run down?'

At that moment the little girl darted from the shadows, almost under the nose of the horse, and pushed Abigail sprawling out of the way. She crashed on what seemed to be wet cobblestones, while the cabbie leant over her and flicked at them both with the tip of his whip, shouting 'Danged baggages! Are ye cracked, standing there like two dummies?'

The cab creaked and clattered onwards. Abigail lay looking up at the lamp. The pedestal was a thick pillar of grooved iron; at the top was a glass-windowed lantern in which waved and waggled a blue fishtail of flame. She had seen pictures of such lamps before, and she knew the light came not from electricity but coal gas.

'Dreaming!' she thought. 'That's all. I'm dreaming.'

But the cobbles were cold and dank, her knees were stinging where she had fallen, the air was full of strange smells, horse manure and tidal flats, wood smoke, human sweat, and an all-pervading odour of sewage.

She felt the little girl withdraw, heard the patter of her bare feet along the road, and panic swept through her.

'Don't leave me – I don't know where I am!'

She scrambled up and ran after the child. Strange, foreign-looking women in long aprons came out of dimly lighted doorways to stare. Children, more dirty and ragged and evil-looking than she had imagined children could be, looked up from floating paper boats in the gutter. One of them threw something stinking at her; it was a rabbit's head, half decayed.

She did not know where she was; all she knew was that the furry little girl might be able to tell her, so she held her skirts up to her knees and ran after her in both terror and desperation.

# Chapter 3

When she thought about it, weeks afterwards, Abigail felt that surely, surely she must have believed herself dreaming for longer than she did. Why didn't I think I'd got into some street where the television people were shooting a film or something? But she knew she hadn't. From the first minute, as she lay dazed on the cobbles, she knew that she was real and the place was real, and so were the people in it.

The furry little girl tried to lose her, ducking up dog-leg courts where the houses pressed close to the earth like lichen. They had shingled roofs covered with moss, and heaps of foul debris around their walls. Sometimes the child glanced over her shoulder as she jumped black gullies of water, or dodged urchins with hair like stiffened mop-heads. Her face was distorted with panic.

The houses were like wasps' nests, or Tibetan houses as Abigail had seen them in films, piled on top of each other, roosting on narrow sandstone ledges, sometimes with a lighted candle stuck in half a turnip on the doorstep, as if to show the way. The dark was coming down, and in those mazy alleys it came quicker. The lamplight that streamed through broken grimy windows was sickly yellow.

The little girl darted past the tall stone cliff of a ware-house, its huge door studded with nail-heads as if against invaders. There Abigail almost caught up with her, but a beggar with a wooden stump reared up and waved his crutch at her, shouting something out of a black toothless mouth. And she saw that she had almost trampled on something she thought was a deformed child, until it leapt snarling to its master's crooked shoulder. It was a monkey in a hussar's uniform.

And now she had gained on the little girl, who was beginning to falter.

They had turned into what Abigail did not immediately recognise as Argyle Street, though she had walked up that street a hundred times. The enormous stone arch of The Cut, the cutting quarried through the sandstone backbone of The Rocks, was different. It was narrower, she thought, though so many shops and stalls and barrows clustered along Argyle Street it was hard to see. Where the Bradfield Highway had roared across the top of The Cut there were now two rickety wooden bridges. Stone steps ran up one side, and on the other two tottering stairways curled upon themselves, overhung with vines and dishevelled trees, and running amongst and even across the roofs of indescribable shanties like broken-down farm sheds. These dwellings were propped up with tree trunks and railway sleepers; goats grazed on their roofs; and over all was the smell of rotting seaweed, ships, wood smoke, human ordure, and horses and harness.

She wondered afterwards why people had stared at her, and realised that it was not because she looked strange – for with her long dress and shawl she was dressed much as they were – but because she was running.

Once a youth with a silly face and a fanciful soldier's uniform, or so she thought, stood in her path, stroking his side whiskers and smirking, but she shoved past him.

Picking out the fugitive child's figure she ran onwards,

almost to the edge of The Cut, where the child dived into a doorway of a corner house or shop, with a lighted window and a smell of burnt sugar that for a moment made her hesitate, for she had smelt it before.

And while she stood there, hesitating, there was a fearful noise within – a feminine protest, the clatter of metal, and a man's angry roar.

Out of the doorway bounded a grotesquely tall figure in a long white apron, brandishing what she thought was a rusty scimitar above his head. He was bellowing something like 'Charge the heathen devils!' as he rushed past her, knocking her down as he went. She hit her head hard on the edge of the doorstep.

The pain was so sharp she was quite blinded. Other people burst from the doorway, there were cries of consternation, and she was lifted to her feet. The pain seemed to move to her ankle, she could see nothing but darkness and lights gone fuzzy and dim.

'I'm awfully sorry,' she whispered. 'I think I'm going to faint.'

When she came to herself, she kept her eyes shut, for she knew very well that she was in neither a hospital nor her own home. The air was warm and stuffy; she thought there was an open fire in the room, and it was burning coal. She knew the smell, for Grandmother had an open fireplace in her house, and burnt coal in winter. Someone was holding her hand. It was a woman's hand, not a child's, though the palm was as hard as a man's. The hand was placed on her forehead for a moment, and a voice, with the accent of the little furry girl's, said softly, 'Aye, she's no' so burning. Change the bandage, Dovey, pet, and we'll see how the dint is.'

Gentle hands touched a tender spot on her head. She managed to keep still, with her eyes shut, partly because

35

she was filled with apprehension at what or whom she might see, and partly because she still felt confused and ill. A distant throb in her ankle grew into a savage pain.

Still she did not believe she was dreaming. She thought, 'I've gone out of my mind in some way; this can't be real, even though it is.'

A girl's voice said, ''Tis clean, Granny, but I'll put a touch of the comfrey paste on it, shall I?'

'Do that, lass, and then you'd best see if your Uncle Samuel is himself again.'

'He's greeting, Beatie said, heartsick at what he did.'

'Poor man, poor man, 'tis an evil I dunna ken the cure for.'

As with the little furry girl, Abigail at first thought these unknown women were speaking some foreign tongue. Then she realised it was an English she had never heard before. She thought, 'Perhaps it's Scots.' After those first bewildered moments, she found that if she listened closely the words began to make sense. She was so desperate to find out where she was, and who these people were, that she concentrated as well as she could on all they said; and after a little, as though she had become accustomed to their speech, their words seemed to turn into under-standable English.

The voices, especially that of the girl, were placid and lilting.

'She's a lady, Granny, no doubt.'

'Aye.'

Abigail felt her hand lifted. Fingers ran over her palm.

'Soft as plush, and will you see the nails? Pink and clean as the Queen's own.'

Abigail's astonishment at this was submerged in a sickening wave of pain from her ankle. Out of her burst a puppy-like yelp of which she was immediately ashamed.

But the pain was too much and she began to sob, 'My foot, my foot!' She opened her eyes and gazed wildly about.

Bending over her was one of the sweetest faces she had ever seen, a young girl's, with a soft, baby's complexion. A horsetail of dull fair hair hung over one shoulder.

'Poor bairnie, poor bairnie. Take a sup of Granny's posset, 'tis so good for pain. There now, all's well, Dovey's here, and Granny, and we'll no' leave you, I promise.'

Granny's posset tasted like parsley, with a bitter after-taste; but although Abigail thought she would instantly be sick she was not. She drifted drowsily away, lulled by the warmth of the fire and the warm hand holding her own.

When she awakened she seemed to be alone. Her clothes had been taken off, and she was wearing a long nightdress of thick hairy material. It had a linen collar that rubbed her neck and chin. She cautiously felt this collar. It had been starched to a papery stiffness. One foot, the painful one, was raised on a pillow. The other was against something hard but comfortingly warm. She felt cautiously around it with her toes.

Then a child's voice said, ''Tis a hot pig you're poking at.'

Abigail snapped open her eyes. Natalie's furry girl sat on a stool beside her, so close that Abigail could see the freckles on her face. Her eyes were excited.

Seeing the child so close was strange but comforting, for she knew this child belonged in her own world; she had seen her and Natalie Crown had seen her. And yet, viewed at close hand, she did not seem like an ordinary little girl at all. There was something headstrong and fierce and resolute in her face. Her little hands were marked with scars and burns.

A wave of intense fright ran over Abigail. The very

37

hairs on her arms prickled. Her breathing became fast. Deep inside her, in her secret place, she began to repeat to herself, 'I mustn't lose hold. I must pretend I haven't noticed anything . . . anything strange.'

Now that her head was no longer whirling, though it was still paining, she was able to collect her thoughts. She didn't like the fact that her clothes had been taken away. She remembered all the stories at school, about girls who were drugged and taken away to South America and Uganda and Algeria to be slaves in terrible places there. Nicole Price absolutely swore on the snippet of Elvis's silk bandanna (which was the most sacred thing in the world to her) that her own cousin had been standing in Castlereagh Street waiting for a bus in broad daylight and was never seen again.

After a while she whispered, 'What's a hot pig?'

'Daftie,' said the girl. ''Tis a stone bottle filled with hot water. Dunna ye ken anything?'

'Why does my foot hurt?' asked Abigail.

'Why wouldn't it? You sprained your ankle terrible bad when you fell.'

Abigail felt a feeble spark of anger. 'I didn't fall. Some great ox knocked me over.' She thought for a while. 'He didn't really . . . really have a sword, did he?'

'Aye, he did. That's me faither. He has spells.'

Abigail thought this over but could make nothing of it. Briefly she thought that if she went to sleep again she might wake up in her own room. But the strong smell of the tallow candle that burnt on the table beside her, the crash of cartwheels and hoofs on the cobbles outside the window, the blast of a ship's whistle from somewhere near, the anxious look of the little girl, denied this.

'What's your name?'

'Beatie Bow.'

38

Abigail scowled. 'Quit having me on, whoever you are. That's the name of a kids' game.'

'I ken that well enough. But it's my name. Beatrice May Bow, and I'm eleven years of age, though small for it, I know, because of the fever.'

Suddenly she gripped Abigail's arm. 'Dunna tell, I'm asking you. Dunna tell Granny where you come from, or I'm for it. She'll say I've the Gift and I havena, and don't want it, God knows, because I'm afeared of what it does.'

Abigail thought muzzily, 'There's some sense in this somewhere, and sooner or later there'll be a clue and I'll understand it.' Aloud she said, 'What *is* this place?'

'It's the best bedroom, and it's in faither's house, behind the confectionery shop.'

'I mean, what country is it?'

The other girl looked flabbergasted. 'Have ye lost your wits? It's the colony of New South Wales.'

Abigail turned her head into the pillow, which was lumpy and smelled puzzlingly of chicken-coops, and sobbed weakly. She understood nothing except that she was hurt, and was afraid to her very toes, and wanted her mother or even her father.

Beatie said urgently, 'Promise you won't tell where you come from. From *there*. I shouldna ha' done it; I were wicked, I know. But when I heard the bairns calling my name, my heart gave a jump like a spring lamb. But I didna mean to bring you here, I didna know it could be done, heaven's truth.'

She was talking riddles. Abigail was frozen with terror. Was she amongst mad people? The memory of some of those terrible hag faces that had confronted her while she was running returned to her – the caved-in mouths, the skin puckered with old blue scars – of what? The fearsome beggar and his wooden leg, a thing shaped like a peg, like

39

Long John Silver's in *Treasure Island*. She gave a loud snuffle of terror.

Beatie shook her, so that her head and her ankle shot forth pangs of agony.

'Promise me or I'll punch ye yeller and green!'

'Leave me alone,' cried Abigail. 'I don't know where I come from, I don't know where this place is, I can't understand anything.'

'You've lost your memory then,' said the little girl with satisfaction. 'Aye, that'll do bonny.'

Abigail trembled. 'Have I? But I remember lots of things: my name, and how old I am, and I live in George Street North, and my mother's name is Kathy, and she's angry with me because . . .' At the thought of her mother, coming home and finding her missing, ringing the police, Dad, being frantic, she lost her head and began to scream. She saw the elder girl limp into the room. Why did she limp? And Beatie Bow looking frightened and defiant.

Then she became aware that a tall old woman stood beside her, holding her hand. She wore a long black dress and white apron, and on her head was a huge pleated white cap with streamers. Afterwards Abigail realised she looked exactly like a fairy godmother, but at the time she thought nothing. She said wonderingly, 'Granny!'

'She's no' your granny, she's ours!' snapped Beatie. Dovey hushed her, smiling.

The old woman put her arms round Abigail, and rocked her against a bosom corseted as hard as a board. Terrified as she was, she was at once aware of the goodness that dwelt in this old woman.

She stole a look upwards, saw the brown skin creased like old silk, a sculptured smile on the sunken mouth. It was a composed, private face, with the lines of hardship and grief written on it.

40

'There, there, lassie, dinna take on so. Granny's here.'

Abigail pressed her face into the black tucked cloth, and held on tight. Something strong and calm radiated from the old woman.

Never in your whole life could you imagine her addressing snide remarks to her bonnet, or the grey silky hair that showed beneath it. She was a real grandmother.

Above her head she heard the grandmother murmur, 'Fetch Judah, Beatie, pet. I think I heard his step. He's that good with bairns.'

'I want my mother,' moaned Abigail.

'Rest sure, my bonnie, that you'll have your mother as soon as we know where she lives, and what you're called.'

A tall young man entered the room. She had a glimpse of fair hair, cut strangely, a square-cut jacket of black or dark blue, with metal buttons, crumpled white trousers.

'Faither's in a state, fair adrift with fright and sorrow. You'd best sit with him, Dovey, till he comes out of it.'

'I'm frightened, I'm frightened,' Abigail whispered.

The young man sat beside her. She could not see his face because the light was in her eyes. Instead she saw a big brown hand, on the outstretched forefinger of which perched a bird as big as a thimble, its feathers a tinsel green.

'Would you know what that is, Eliza?'

'My name isn't Eliza,' whispered Abigail, 'it's Abigail. And that's a humming-bird. But it isn't alive, it's stuffed.'

The young man stroked the tiny glittering head with one finger.

'She came from the Orinoco. I got her for a florin from a deepwater man. Did ye ever see aught as fine?'

He turned the finger this way and that, and the little bird shone like an emerald.

'Will you listen to the way she speaks,' murmured the

41

old woman to Beatie. 'I fear your dada will be in desperate trouble if he's injured her, for she's a lady.'

'I'm not a lady,' muttered Abigail. 'I'm just a girl. *You're* a lady.'

'Not me, child,' said the old woman. 'Why, we Talliskers have been fisherfolk since the Earls of Stewart.'

Abigail could make no sense of any of it. She buried her face in the chickeny pillow. Maybe when she opened her eyes again she would be in her own bed, her own bedroom. But clearly she heard the young man blowing up the fire. It was with a bellows. She knew the rhythmic wheeze, for bellows were a popular item at Magpies. There! She remembered Magpies, even where things were put; Mum's crazy sixty-year-old cash register with all the beautiful bronze-work, the green plush tablecloth draped over the delicate rattan whatnot.

She forced her eyes open. The room was now much brighter. The firelight leapt up, reflecting pinkly on a sloping ceiling. On the table was now a tall oil lamp, and Dovey was carefully turning down the wick.

There was a marble wash-stand in the corner, with a blue flowered thick china wash-basin set into a recess. Underneath stood a tall fluted water jug, and a similarly patterned chamber-pot. The fireplace had an iron hob and on it was a jug of what Abigail thought, from the delicious smell, was hot cocoa. The jug was large and white, and in an oval of leaves was imprinted the face of a youngish man with long dark silky whiskers. She had seen him before in Magpies, too.

'That's Prince Albert, isn't it?' she asked.

'Yes, God rest him. He was taken too soon,' replied the old woman.

Judah brought something out of his pocket and proffered

it to her on the palm of his brown hand. It was a pink sugar mouse.

'Our faither makes them. Do you fancy a nibble?'

Abigail did not even see it. She sat shakily up in bed. She saw over the mantel a picture of a middle-aged woman in black, with a small coronet over a white lace veil.

How many times had Abigail seen that sulky, solemn face – on china, miniatures, christening mugs?

'Why ever have you a picture of old Victoria on the wall?' she asked.

'You mustn't speak of our gracious Queen in that way, child!' said Granny severely.

'But our queen is Elizabeth!'

They laughed kindly. 'Why, good Queen Bess died hundreds of years ago, lass. You're still wandering a little; but don't fret: tomorrow you'll be as good as gold.'

Abigail said nothing more. She stared at Queen Victoria in her black widow's weeds and her jet jewellery. Once again, deep inside her, she was saying, 'I must be calm. There's some explanation. I mustn't give myself away.'

Out in the darkness she could hear ships baa-ing on the harbour. 'Is it foggy?' she asked.

'Aye, so maybe I won't be leaving in the morn,' said Judah. 'I'm a seaman, you see, lass.'

Quite near by a bell blommed slow and stately. Abigail jumped.

'It's naught but St Philip's ringing for evensong,' said Dovey softly. 'Ah, she's all of a swither with the shock she got when Uncle Samuel ran into her, poor lamb.'

Abigail tried to still her quaking body. She said to the young man, 'I want to see where I am. Would you help me to the window?'

43

'Sure as your life, hen,' replied the young fellow heartily. Abigail had expected only to lean on his arm, but he gathered her up, bedclothes and all, and took her to the window. He had the same dark-blue eyes as the old woman.

'What are ye girning about, Beatie?' he chided. 'Open the shutters, lass.'

Sulkily and unwillingly, the little girl unlatched the shutters and threw them wide. Abigail looked out on a gas-lit street, fog forming ghostly rainbows about the lamps. A man pushed a barrow on which glowed a brazier. 'Hot chestnuts, all hot, all hot!' His shout came clearly to Abigail. Women hurried past, all with shawls, some with men's caps pulled over their hair, others with large battered hats with tattered feathers.

But Abigail was looking for something else. She was upstairs, she knew, above the confectionery shop, and she had a wide view of smoking chimneys, hundreds, thousands of smoking chimneys, it seemed, each with a faint pink glow above it.

Mitchell should have been standing there, lit like a Christmas tree at this time of night. The city should have glittered like a galaxy of stars. The city was still there – she could see dimmish blotches of light, and vehicles that moved very slowly and bumpily.

'The Bridge has gone, too,' she whispered. No broad lighted deck strode across the little peninsula, no great arch with its winking ruby at the highest point – nothing. The flower-like outline of the Opera House was missing.

She turned her face against Judah's chest and buried it so deeply that she could even hear his heart thumping steadily.

'What is it, Abby? What ails you, child?'

44

For the first time she looked into his face. It was brown and ruddy, a snubbed, country kind of face.

'What year is this?' she whispered.

He looked dumbfounded. 'Are you codding me?'

'What year is it?' she repeated.

'Why, it's 1873, and most gone already,' he said.

Abigail said no more. He took her back to the bed, and Dovey gently folded the covers over her.

'It's true then,' she said uneasily to the old grandmother. 'She's lost her memory. Dear God, what will we do, Granny? For 'twas Uncle Samuel that caused it, and in all charity we've the responsibility of her.'

The tall old woman murmured something. Abigail caught the word 'stranger . . .'

Dovey looked dubious. 'It's my belief she's an immigrant lass, sent to one of the fine houses on the High Rocks to be a parlourmaid, perhaps, for she speaks so bonny. Not like folk hereabouts at all! But where's her traps, do you think, Granny? Stolen or lost? Just what she stood up in, and the Dear knows there was little enough of that!'

Thus they talked in low voices beside the door, while Beatie Bow crept a little closer and stared with thrilled yet terrified eyes at Abigail.

'You!' said Abigail in a fierce whisper. 'You did this to me!'

''Tisn't so,' objected Beatie. 'You chased me up alley and down gully, like a fox after a hare. It wunna my fault!'

Abigail was silent. She kept saying to herself, 'Abigail Kirk, that's who I am. I mustn't forget. I might sink down and get lost in this place – this time, or whatever it is – if I don't keep my mind on it.'

Judah and Granny had gone down the stairs. Dovey limped over and put a hand on Abigail's forehead. 'You've no fever, and the ankle will be a wee bit easier tomorrow. You stay here and talk to Abby, Beatie, seeing that you're getting on so grand, and I'll heat up some broth for your supper.'

Beatie stared at Abigail crossly, defiantly, and yet with anxiety.

'It'd be no skin off your nose if you codded you'd lost your memory because of that dint on the head. I dunna want my granny to know.'

'I want to go back to my own place,' said Abigail in a hard voice.

'I dunna ken where your ain place is,' protested Beatie. 'I didna mean to go there myself. It were the bairnies calling my name. I dunna ken how I did it, honest. I never did it afore I had the fever.'

As though to herself, in a puzzled, worried voice she said, 'One minute I was in the lane, and the next there was a wall there, and the bairnies skittering about, and all those places like towers and castles and that . . . that great road that goes over the water, and strange carriages on it with never a horse amongst them, and I was afeared out of my wits, thinking the fever had turned my brain. And then I heard children calling my name, and they were playing a game we play around the streets here, except that we call it Janey Jo. But they couldna see me, because I tried to speak to one or two. Only you and that wee little one with the yellow coat.'

The child's cocky attitude had vanished. Her face was sallow and the big hollow eyes shone. Abigail remembered that Natalie had wept because she believed that this girl had been unhappy. She had mentioned fever. Perhaps that was why Beatie's hair had been cut so short. Abigail remembered that once it had been the custom to shave the heads of fever patients. She was about to ask about

46

this, when Beatie said in an awed voice, 'Is it Elfland, that place where you come from?'

'Of course it isn't, there isn't any Elfland. Are you crazy?'

Beatie said in a hushed voice. 'Green as a leek, you are. Of course there's Elfland. Isn't that where Granny's great-great-granny got the Gift, the time she was lost so long?'

'You're crazy,' said Abigail. 'You're all crazy.'

She closed her eyes. The fire crackled, the room was full of strange smells, but the smell of burnt sugar was strongest of all. A hand timidly touched hers.

'It's bonny.'

'What is?'

'That place you were. Elfland.'

Abigail opened her eyes and glared into the tawny ones. 'I told you it wasn't Elfland.'

'Where is it then?'

'Guess,' said Abigail snappily.

Beatie Bow was silent. Abigail stared at the ceiling. Then Beatie Bow said, 'How did those children know my name?'

'I wouldn't know, and if I did I wouldn't tell you.'

She wanted to scream like a seagull. With a great effort she kept the sounds of lostness and fright down in her chest. Her head was throbbing again and her ankle felt like a bursting football.

'If it wasna Elfland,' said Beatie slowly and thoughtfully, 'it was some place I dunna ken about. Yet the bairns there don't play Janey Jo any more; they play Beatie Bow.'

Abigail didn't answer.

Suddenly the little girl shouted, 'I will make you tell, I will! I want to know about the castles and palaces, and the lights that went so fast, and the queer old things the

47

bairns were playing on, and how they knew my name. I'll punch ye yeller and green, I swear it, if ye dunna tell!'

'Maybe you've got the Gift,' said Abigail cruelly. Beatie turned so white her freckles seemed twice as numerous. Abigail said, 'You get me back there where I met you, or I'll tell your granny where I come from and who brought me.'

Beatie whipped up a hard little fist as though to clout her.

'I dunna want the Gift. I'm feared of it! I wunna have it!'

Abigail thought hazily, 'When I get back home, or wake up, or whatever I'm going to do, I'll be sorry I didn't ask her what this stupid Gift is. But just now I don't care.'

She turned away from Beatie's anxious, angry face, and pretended to be asleep. Within a moment or two she was.

# Chapter 4

Twice during the night Abigail awakened to hear a child whimpering forlornly somewhere above the ceiling.

'That can't be,' she thought muzzily. Then she remembered that this was an old-fashioned house. There might be attics.

Dovey had left the lamp turned low. The round glass globe had bunches of grapes etched on it. The fire had gone out and there was a smell of cold ashes.

She heard a halting step on stairs somewhere. So there really must be yet another child, and Dovey was coming down from looking after it.

Abigail didn't know whether she liked Dovey or not. She seemed so gentle and good, but Abigail knew from books and TV that an angelic exterior often hid an interior chock-full of black evil. Besides, she didn't want to be comforted by Dovey at two in the morning or whatever it was; so as the girl limped into the room Abigail pretended to be asleep. Dovey wore a baggy red-flannel dressing-gown, and her hair was in a plait tied with a scrap of wool. She looked worn and sleepy.

Granny was with her in an even baggier red-flannel dressing-gown. Her hair was tucked under what Abigail imagined was a nightcap, a little baby bonnet with a frill about the face, and tapes under the chin.

'The hideous clothes the Victorian working class wore,'

marvelled Abigail – a long way from the hailstone muslin and exquisite China silks that sometimes ended up at Magpies.

'Did Judah get away, hen?' asked Granny.

'Aye. He'll sleep on board, for the fog's lifting and he thought the skipper'd be away with the morn's tide. I gave Gibbie a draught and he's asleep, but he looks poorly, Granny. Do you have a good or a bad feeling about him, poor bairn?'

Granny sighed. 'I hae no clear feelings any more, Dovey. They're as mixed up as folk in fog.'

'But you've no doubt that this little one here is the Stranger?'

The two women spoke in whispers, but Abigail heard them, for the night was almost silent. There was no sound of traffic except a dray's wheels rolling like distant thunder over the cobbles at the docks. She could hear the waves breaking on the rocks of Dawes Point and Walsh Bay.

'Aye, when I first saw her I had a flash, clear as it was when I was a lass. Poor ill-favoured little yellow herring of a thing. But still, it came to me then, she was the Stranger that would save the Gift for the family.'

Abigail was so indignant at the description of herself that she almost opened her eyes.

'And then there was the gown, forebye. I swear, Granny, I almost fainted when I set eyes on it. The very pattern that we worked out between us!'

'And not a needle lifted to it yet,' said Granny. 'Hush, Dovey, the child is stirring.'

The lamp's reflections on the ceiling shifted, and the room was left in darkness. Abigail had the impression that Dovey came back to sleep in the other bed, but she was unable to keep awake to see.

'I'll bet I've had one of Granny's possets in the cocoa or something. On top of everything else they'll poison me.'

This was her last outraged thought as she sank into sleep. She was still resentful when she awoke. The trundle-bed had been slept in but was unoccupied; the house was full of unfamiliar noises, metal clinking vigorously (the fire downstairs being raked out?), the continuous puling complaint from above (the mysterious Gibbie?), someone yelling in a temper (Beatie, without a doubt), and Granny's soft full tones, making peace amongst them all.

She struggled to a sitting position. Her head felt better, clearer. Her ankle still hurt frightfully. She peeled back the bedclothes to look at it. Hideous! Yellow and purple and swollen to twice its size. But perhaps it wasn't as painful as yesterday.

'Now then,' thought Abigail, inside this new clear head, 'something very weird has happened to me. I'm in the last century. I don't know why, and that doesn't matter. I've got to get back, before Mum goes mad with worry. Dad, too, I suppose. Now, what were those women talking about last night when they thought I was asleep?'

She concentrated. Some of the words came back.

'I didn't dream them. Granny said I was the Stranger, without doubt. Well, I'm a stranger all right, but what's *the* Stranger? And there was that other bit about saving the Gift for the family. This creepy Gift that Beatie's always sounding off about.

'Then they said something about my dress, my Edwardian dress.'

She was puzzling her head over the half-remembered words when Dovey entered with a metal can full of steaming water.

She poured it in the basin on the wash-stand.

51

'How do you feel this morning, Abby love?'

'Better,' said Abby. 'I want to get up. I think I can hop around.'

'We'll ask Granny first.' Dovey smiled. 'Can you remember anything more clear-like today?'

Abigail was about to tell her snippily that she had never forgotten anything at all, but caution kept her silent. She said, 'I'm Abigail Kirk, and I'm fourteen.'

'Never!' said Dovey, astonished. 'I'd thought you about our Beatie's age. Why, you've not filled out in the least.'

Abigail thought bitterly of the 'little yellow herring of a thing' but kept her thoughts to herself. She said with false wistfulness, 'It's a pity, but none of my fault.'

'Perhaps you were not well fed as a babby,' said Dovey sympathetically, briskly washing Abigail down to the waist.

'They've no business sending you out to a situation, under-sized as you are. There now, put on your shift, hen, and I'll give your legs a rub.'

'Can't I have my own clothes?' asked Abigail. 'Where's my dress?'

Dovey looked uncomfortable. A rosebud blush crept over her china-like complexion. 'I believe 'twas so stained with blood and dirt Granny burnt it.'

'But it was new and I loved it,' wailed Abigail. Just in time she clamped her mouth shut. Don't talk. Just listen. You have to be sharper than these people, nice as they seem to be, or you'll never get home.

'It was my best,' she said chokily.

'Ne'er mind,' Dovey said soothingly. 'I've a skirt and bodice you can wear and welcome. But first we must let Granny see if you're well enough to come downstairs.'

Granny said no. She said after a dint on the head-bone rest was necessary.

'But I've nothing to do,' complained Abigail. 'Isn't there anything I can read?'

Dovey and Granny exchanged pleased glances. 'So you can read, lass? Can you figure, too?'

In her astonishment Abigail almost laughed, but she lowered her eyes and said, 'Well enough.'

'In our family we have considerable learning,' said Granny with quiet pride, 'for we had the advantage of a grand dominie back home in Orkney. But here in the colony poor Beatie and Gibbie, who's the wean that's still sickly from the fever that carried off his mother and her babe – they've naught but the Ragged School. And that's no' good enough for Talliskers, even though it may be so for Bows.'

'Now, Granny,' objected Dovey mildly. ''Tisn't Uncle Samuel's fault he can sign his name only with a cross. To be sore wounded for his country's sake is more than enough to ask of a sojer.'

But there was nothing for Abigail to read except the family Bible, and to this she shook her head.

'You're never godless?' asked Granny anxiously. After some thought Abigail understood she was asking about religion.

'I don't remember,' she whispered.

'Poor bairnie,' said Granny. 'Dovey, send Beatie to her when she comes from school, to speak to her of Scripture. It may bring the child's memories back to her. Not to remember our Father in Heaven!'

At the thought of her own father, Abigail's eyes filled with genuine tears. Oh, what was he doing? Thinking her kidnapped or murdered, comforting her mother or blaming her for letting her go home alone?

'Be brave, lass,' said Granny. 'You can do no less.'

Abigail looked blurrily at the strong clear-cut features

of the old woman. 'All right for you,' she thought; 'you aren't desperate like me.'

While she lay there the sounds of the nineteenth-century Rocks rose up from out of the street, horses slipping and sliding on slimy cobbles, a refrain from a concertina, market cries: 'Tripe, all 'ot and juicy! Cloes prarps! Windsor apples! Rag 'n' bones, bring 'em out! China pears! Lamp oil, cheapest in town!'

From somewhere near the water came the sweetly harsh summons of a bugle. 'That'll be the Dawes Point Battery,' thought Abigail, marvelling. 'Fancy – real live troops there, and muskets and drums! And all I've ever seen in my time are bits of old wall, and the cannons, and grass, and people sitting under the Bridge eating their lunches.'

Disagreeable things happened to her. She had to use the chamber-pot, while Dovey bustled around tossing up her pillows and pulling the coverlet straight. Of course, it had to be done. Abigail realised that the lavatory, if there was one, would be a little shed at the bottom of the yard, with a can and a wooden seat with a hole in it. But even though Dovey was matter-of-fact about it, Abigail hated it.

To keep her mind off her embarrassment she thought how much her mother would enjoy seeing Dovey. She was so like one of the Victorian china dolls that sold for huge prices at Magpies that Abigail wondered if the dolls' faces hadn't been modelled on those of real girls. She had a tiny chin with a dent in it, blue eyes that Abigail thought bulgy, and a little soft neck with circular wrinkles running around it.

Her real name was Dorcas Tallisker, and she limped because when they were young Judah had run over the cliff with her in a trundle-cart and her thigh-bone had been broken. Sometimes it stiffened up, and then she had

54

to walk with a stick; but the warm New South Wales weather had made the pain lessen.

'The Orkney isles are harsh country,' she said, 'for all there is such beauty there – the heather, and the wild birds crying, and the great craigs and the magic stones.'

'Magic stones?' asked Abigail.

'Aye,' said Dovey simply. 'Built by dwarfies, ye ken, and even giants so they say, long before the Northmen came; for Orkney folk is half Scots and half Norwegian, so 'tis said. Ah, I would that I was there now, milking my wee cow Silky.'

Sad of face, she helped Abigail back to bed and went away with the chamber-pot covered with a cloth. Soon she was back with a little brass shovel with a few red hot coals upon it. Abigail watched with interest as Dovey put sprigs of dried lavender on the coals and waved the resultant thin blue smoke about the room.

'There now! You're all sweet again.'

'Can't I have the window open?' asked Abigail.

Dovey was shocked. 'But the spring air brings so many fluxes and congestions in the chest,' she said. 'And you're still no' yourself, ye ken, Abby.'

So it was spring. But how? For when she had left home it was already lowering with winter. She recalled how Beatie, in her thin dress and shawl, had shuddered with cold.

How could it be? Where had all the time gone?

But she was unable to puzzle further, because footsteps came up the stairs. Dovey, brushing Abigail's hair, hastily pulled the sheet up to her neck, so that she would look proper, and said, "Tis Uncle Samuel. Try to forgive him for the harm he did you, love, for, as you'll see, he's a pitiful man.'

The tall man who came stooping through the little

55

doorway was stooped and spindly himself. He was the ruin of what had probably been a handsome trooper in his blue and buff uniform and pipe-clayed gaiters. His ashy hair looked as if it had flour in it, and his bright blue eyes were spectacularly crossed.

''Tis the effect of the head wound,' murmured Dovey. She said in a louder voice, 'Come in, Uncle Samuel. Abigail is much better today.'

Mr Bow wore a long white apron. He smelt deliciously of syrup and almonds. He twisted his scarred hands in his apron and said abjectly, 'Oh, dear Miss, there hain't words to tell how broken up I am for doin' yer such damage. It's these spells, you see. I think I'm back at Balaclava and I hain't seein' a thing but Rooshians like bears in their big coats. And I pray from the bottom of me heart, honest to God, that I didn't do yer too much harm.'

Abigail was much taken with Mr Bow. He looked so much like a Siamese cat. She could see Beatie's little face scowling from under his arm.

'It wasn't your fault, Mr Bow. I just didn't get out of the way quickly enough. And all I have are a sprained ankle and a bump on the head, so you've nothing to worry about.'

'You're sartin sure you forgive me?' he asked pleadingly. 'I hain't been myself since my dear 'Melia died, you see, and then when Granny tells me you're the Stranger . . .'

'Hush, Dada!' said Beatie, and the tall man, mopping his eyes, turned, muttering, 'Ah, she was a good wife, my 'Melia, and the babby, such a fine sonsy lad – make two of Gibbie, he would.'

As he went out, Beatie dawdled in and gave Abby a sullen look.

'Did you do well at school today, hen?' asked Dovey.

'Patching,' Beatie said scornfully, 'and how to curtsey

56

when the Lady Visitor came. And I was sore scolded for wearing no shoes. The Lady Visitor said I might as well be a Chinaman.'

'Indeed!' exclaimed Dovey. Bright scarlet stained her cheeks. 'We'll do something about that. Orkney folk are not to be spoken to in such a way, I tell you. But I'll not soil myself with anger at such trash. Beatie, lass, Granny wants you to read the Gospel to Abby, for she's no memory of the Lord's good words, either.'

From the tall narrow cupboard she took a huge book bound in half-bald green plush, its edges reinforced with well-polished brass.

'The Sermon on the Mount would be a bonny choice,' she said. 'And now I'll see to Gibbie. Granny's been up with him half the night.'

Beatie grimaced at Abigail. 'I'd liefer read the bloody bits, about slaughtering the enemy and blowing down walls and sticking pikes into the Canaanites.'

'Save your breath,' said Abigail briskly. She pulled herself up on her pillows. 'I want to talk to you.'

'If you're about to ask me to take you back where I got you, you can save your ain breath,' snapped Beatie, 'because I don't know how to do it, and that's the truth of it.'

The two girls glared at each other. Then Abigail laughed. The younger child was such a fierce homely creature, the eyes so bright and intelligent, the small thin hands crooked as though they would claw the eyes out of life itself.

'You've got plenty of brains,' said Abigail.

'Aye,' said Beatie suspiciously. 'And what brings you to say that?'

'Because I think you want to do other things besides learn how to feather-stitch and drop curtseys to rude rich old hags at the Ragged School.'

57

Beatie's tawny eyes glittered. 'True enough. I want to learn Greek and Latin like the boys. And geography. And algebra. And yet I'll never. Gibbie will learn them afore me, and he's next door to a mumblepate!'

'But why?' asked Abigail.

'Why, why?' cried Beatie. 'Because I'm a girl, that's why, and girls canna become scholars. Not unless their fathers are rich, and most of *their* daughters are learnt naught but how to dabble in paints, twiddle on the pianoforte, and make themselves pretty for a good match!'

Suddenly light broke upon Abigail. 'So that's why you wanted to know why the children were playing Beatie Bow, how they got to know about you?'

'That's what I asked before,' answered Beatie resentfully, 'an' ye wunna tell me, damn ye!'

'Well, I don't truly know,' said Abigail, 'but I think I can guess.'

'Tell me!' cried Beatie, bright-eyed.

'We'll trade,' said Abigail.

'I dinna know what you mean,' said Beatie suspiciously.

'You say you can't get me back to where I came from. Maybe that's true. But could you help me to Harrington Street? Because that's where things started to change. And maybe if I got back there . . .'

'I could. But it wunna be easy because Granny thinks you're none other than . . .' Beatie stopped short.

'I know. The Stranger, whatever that is. But will you help me get to Harrington Street, when my ankle's a little better?'

'I dinna like going agin Granny,' muttered Beatie. 'She's got the Gift. It's not what it was when she was a lass, but she's still got powers.'

'Very well, then. Go away,' said Abigail, and she lay down and turned her back on Beatie. She heard the child

58

fidgeting around, going to the door once or twice, then coming back hesitantly to stand beside the bed.

'Right, I'll help you, and the dear God help me if Granny kens what I'm doing, for she's dead set on your staying. There, I've given my word. Now for your part of the bargain.'

Abigail sat up again. 'I think those children were using your name in their game because you got to be famous.'

Beatie's face flushed. 'Me? You're daft. Famous? In Elfland?'

'It isn't Elfland,' said Abigail, exasperated. 'How many more times? If I tell you where . . . what . . . that place is, do you solemnly swear it will be our secret?'

'I swear,' said Beatie. 'I swear by my mother's grave, and there inna anything in the world more sacred than that.'

So Abigail told her. The little girl burst into wrathful indignation.

'You ought to be ashamed, telling me such lees. You'll go to hell for it, and be toasted on a pitchfork!'

'You saw it for yourself,' said Abigail, taken aback, 'the Bridge and the Opera House, and all the tall buildings. Why, I live in one of them, right at the top!'

'You're a damned leear. Such things inna possible except in Elfland.' But the girl's voice quavered.

'I wouldn't have thought this place, time, or whatever it is, would be possible either,' Abigail said angrily.

'What's the matter with here then?' shouted Beatie in a whisper.

'For one thing, it stinks like a pig-pen, and for another they won't let a girl have a proper education, and for another people can die here of fever, and smallpox, and diphtheria.'

Beatie was silent. Then she said hoarsely, 'Don't folk

59

die of those things in . . . that time?' When Abigail shook her head, Beatie broke into a passion of sobbing. 'Then Mamma would still be alive, and the babby, and Gibbie wouldn't be so sickly.'

Abigail let her sob. Suddenly she felt towards this wounded tough little scrap as she had felt towards Natalie in that other life. But she did not touch her. She knew instinctively that Beatie would throw off any sympathetic hand.

At last Beatie was silent.

'I thought I was over it,' she said in a stifled voice.

'You will be some day.'

'It wunna lees you told me, then?'

'No,' said Abigail. 'But I want to get back as soon as I can walk properly because my mother and father will be anxious to death about me.'

Beatie nodded. 'I know how you feel about your mother. When I cried when Mamma was dying, Dovey said "Dunna let her go to her reward fretting about you, child" – that's what she said. "For Granny and I are here to look after you and Gib. I'll be your mother, hen," she said. "Smile now and let your mamma be at ease." So I did.'

She was quiet for a while, sniffling. Then she said grudgingly, 'You're no' so bad, you.'

'Neither are you,' said Abigail, grinning. 'Is it a bargain then?'

Beatie stuck out her hard, work-harsh little fist and they shook hands.

During the next two days Abigail learnt a great deal about these people amongst whom she had been thrown in such a strange way. She learnt that the Orkneys were a hard and ancient group of islands set amongst dangerous seas north of Scotland. All of the family had been born there except Mr Bow the Englishman, Gibbie, and the baby boy who had died with his mother.

Dorcas Tallisker was the cousin of the Bows. Her mother had died when she was born, and she was reared by her fisherman father Robert Tallisker, and his mother, Granny. Two years before, Dovey's father was drowned in a squall in Hoy Sound, off Stromness, and Granny had decided to emigrate to New South Wales to live with her daughter, Amelia, who had married an English soldier, Samuel Bow. When Dovey and Granny arrived, they found Amelia, the children Beatie and Gilbert, and a six-months-old infant, deathly ill with the fever.

'What kind of fever?' thought Abigail uneasily, remembering that though she had been immunised against most modern infectious diseases, a dockside area of the 1870s very likely had plenty of lethal bugs of its own.

'The typhoid,' said Beatie. ''Tis very common in these parts.'

Abigail decided she'd drink nothing but tea. At least she would know the water had been boiled.

'And now tell me about the Gift,' she said. Beatie gave her a scared look.

'No, I wunna. Granny would ne'er forgive me. It's the family Gift, you see.'

'But I'm connected with it in some way. I'm the Stranger. Even your father said so. I ought to know what it is; it's my right. Tell me or I'll ask Granny.'

'Dunna,' pleaded the child. 'I'm gey scared of it, Abby. I dunna want it. I just want to be a scholar. I dunna want to see things and know things a mortal body shouldna know.'

'Why,' Abigail thought, 'it's the second sight, ESP, or

61

something. And Beatie's afraid that she might have it too, poor brat.'

But she said nothing.

By the third day she was allowed to get dressed and be carried downstairs by Mr Bow. In fact she was dressed by Dovey: for when confronted with the garments the older girl lent her she had not the faintest idea how to put them on. There was a boned bodice of stiff calico fastened with rows of strong hooks and eyes at the back. Abigail eyed it with distaste.

'Where's my own underwear?' she demanded.

'But you had hardly a thing for underclothes,' answered Dovey. 'Just a few queer rags and drawers the size of a baby's. Now, slip your arms through here, and I'll hook you up, and you'll be more comfortable.'

Scowling, Abigail did so. She also obediently drew on the cotton knickers and the long flannel ones that went over them, a waist petticoat that tied with a tape, and a woollen blouse that had long full sleeves and did up to the neck with an endless row of pearl buttons.

'She's such a skinny wee thing she won't need the stays, Granny,' said Dovey. Abigail thanked heaven.

'I'm boiling,' she said. 'I don't wear heavy clothes like this, ever!'

''Tis the kind of clothes worn at this season,' said Granny with her quiet inflexibility, 'and Dovey's best, at that.'

'I do thank you,' said Abigail awkwardly, 'but it's not what I'm used to, you see.'

When she was completely dressed, in a long dark serge skirt over the blouse, a ribbon belt with a pewter buckle, knee-high stockings of hand-knitted wool in circles of brown and yellow, and one of Granny's best buttoned boots (for Dovey had feet as tiny as her hands, and her boots would not fit Abigail by three sizes) on her good leg, she felt like a wooden image, stiff, clumsy, and half choked with the smell of mothballs and lavender that drifted from the fabric. On her other foot she had a knitted slipper with a fringed top. She hopped over to the mirror and recoiled.

'I never saw such a scarecrow in my life!'

She looked so hideous she could have cried. But she had finished with crying; and, anyway, she couldn't afford to lose her eyes as well.

'You'll look more yourself when your hair is brushed,' said Dovey in her soothing way. She brushed Abigail's hair flat off her forehead and plaited it tightly from the nape of her neck. The corners of Abigail's eyes were pulled taut, so that she looked like a beaten-up Oriental. A huge greenish-blue bruise extended from her forehead to her cheek. Her nose had become pointy, and her teeth seemed to stick out.

'Dracula teeth,' she said mournfully, then hurriedly covered her slip by murmuring, 'I look so awful!'

'Beauty does not matter. It is all vanity, the Good Book says,' reproved Dovey gently.

'No wonder people in Victorian photographs look so monstrous,' thought Abigail. 'They didn't have a chance, what with no make-up, ugly hair-dos and clothes that would make the skinniest woman look like a haystack.'

Mr Bow carried her downstairs. He seemed silent and absent-minded. There was a peculiar dull sheen in his eyes, and a red patch on each cheek.

Downstairs the odours of sweet-making were strong. Abigail could smell aniseed, treacle, hot butter, and boiling sugar.

She said, 'I'd so like to see the shop, Mr Bow.' But he did not seem to hear.

63

'I bet he's working up to another spell,' she thought uneasily. Being so close to his head she could see the old wound in his skull, a scarred hole only half covered by the ashy grey hair. It was so big she could have laid the fingers of one hand in it. She shuddered and looked away.

'What did they fight with in that Crimean War? Axes?' she wondered. 'How it must have hurt!'

He carried her into the little front room. A small fire burnt in the basket grate. The furniture, covered with rose-patterned plush and stuffed as hard as bricks with horsehair, was plainly not for sitting on. Abigail was placed in a rocking-chair to one side of the fireplace. ('As if I were one of a pair of china dogs,' she thought later.) On the other side, in a smaller rocking-chair, swathed in shawls, was a small peaky-faced boy.

'I'm Gilbert Samuel Bow,' he announced in an important and yet tremulous voice, 'and I'm in a decline. But if I live to my next birthday I'll be ten.'

Abigail looked at him with distaste. She felt like saying, 'Why bother?' But Dovey was hovering around, so she didn't.

# Chapter 5

Gibbie peered out of his huddle of shawls like a small wizened monk. His head had been shaved. It was not an agreeable head, being bony, bumpy, and bluish.

'Mercy on us!' piped this monkish person. 'You're as plain as a toad.'

'Thanks very much,' said Abigail, nettled. 'You're not exactly a dazzler yourself.'

The little face assumed an expression of insufferable piety. 'I expect you know I'm not long for this world. I've been given up by the doctors.'

Dovey limped in with two bowls of broth on a tray and a box of dominoes.

'Just to pass the time away,' she said coaxingly. Gibbie turned up his eyes and said, 'I mun turn away from the things of this world.'

'Oh, fiddlesticks!' growled Abigail. 'You'd get better faster if you moved yourself out in the sun and fresh air, instead of lying around like an old granny.'

Dovey reproved her. 'Gibbie has been nigh to death, Abby,' she said.

Gibbie put on a holy face. 'And I still am. Maybe by my birthday I shall be with my mamma and the angels in heaven.'

Abigail looked disgusted. It seemed to her that a good spank on the backside would do wonders for this whiney, self-important little monster. She marvelled at Dovey's patience with him. Typical Victorian morbidity about the sick and the dead, she thought, remembering what her mother had said about this mildewed aspect of the Victorian era. Certainly kilos of 'mourning' stuff came into Magpies – jet jewellery; brooches containing wreaths of the dear departed's hair; once an onyx-framed miniature topped with two delightful tiny weeping angels. The miniature was of a white-eyed gentleman with side-whiskers and carnation cheeks. It had gone off, to the accompaniment of shrieks of laughter, as a conversation piece. At the time Abigail had thought the buyer's mirth unbearably vulgar; because, after all, that man had once been real and someone had loved him and missed him when he died.

But now, in the middle of it all, and real as she was, all she could feel was exasperation and grumpiness. It was partly because she wasn't as clean as she was used to being. She loathed this. Her hair was lank and greasy. That morning she had asked Dovey if she could wash it in the bathroom and the elder girl had gazed at her in innocent dismay.

'But there's no such place, Abby love, only in the grand houses!'

Abigail, who was accustomed to dashing under the shower whenever she felt like it, was aghast.

'But however do you keep clean?'

Dovey explained that on Saturday nights Granny and the girls bathed in front of the bedroom fire. Uncle Samuel brought up the wooden tub and the hot water, and emptied it afterwards.

'The menfolk wash in front of the kitchen fire, do you see? But it must be on Saturday, so as to be clean and proper for the Sabbath.'

'But your clothes, how do you wash them?' asked Abigail.

Dovey said, a little indignantly, 'Our linen is boiled in the downstairs copper every Monday, rain or shine, and hung out to bleach in the yard. And our outer clothes are sponged regular every month with vinegar or ivy water, which is a fine cleanser, and better than the ammonia some use. Oh, we keep good and cleanly, have no fear of that!'

'Oh, sugar!' thought Abigail in despair. 'No wonder everyone whiffs like an old dishcloth.'

It had never occurred to her that manufacturers would actually produce a fabric that couldn't be washed or dry-cleaned (though she supposed the vinegar and ivy-water, whatever that was, was a kind of dry-or-damp cleaning). Probably Granny's black linsey-wool dress had never had a wash in its life, though it smelt clean enough – if you liked the smell of camphor and lavender water, that is.

'Well,' she thought, 'I've just got to get used to it – even beastly grubby hair. Just fancy what these people would think of drip-dry clothes!'

'Ye hae'na noticed I haven't touched a sip of ma broth,' complained Gibbie.

Abigail, who had eaten hers enthusiastically, for she felt hungry this last day or two, said, 'Too bad for you. It's good.'

'I been thinking on my funeral,' Gibbie said pleasurably. 'Six black horses I'll have, with plumes, and four men in tall hats with black streamers and a dead cart covered in flowers. But my coffin will be white because I'm just an innocent child.'

Abigail looked at him both amused and revolted. 'You want to get those ideas out of your head, you silly little twit, or you *will* die. And then think how sad Granny and Dovey and Judah and Beatie will be.'

'Aye,' said Gibbie with satisfaction, 'they'll greet and groan for a month.'

Abigail shook her head disbelievingly. She would never have thought there could be a child as repellent as Vincent Crown, but Gibbie had him licked into a cocked hat. However, she thought she'd better try to do what she could for him, so she said cheerfully, 'Bet I can beat you at dominoes.'

'It's evil to gamble,' said Gibbie, shocked.

'Holy snakes!' protested Abigail. 'Who's going to gamble?'

Gibbie shrank back. 'You *blasphemed*,' he gasped.

'Oh, for heaven's sake, I'm sick of you, you little creep,' said Abigail. She went to the window. There was no doubt, her ankle felt stronger.

'If only I could go barefoot,' she thought, for Granny's best boot felt terrible. The heel was the wrong height, the upper nipped cruelly at the instep, and the toe was pointed like a dachshund's nose.

'You must be from a foreign land, as Dovey said,' observed Gibbie. 'You canna speak proper English like the rest of us, poor soul.'

'Who's talking?' asked Abigail. She pulled the dusty brown curtains aside.

Behind them was a little window made of six square glass panes, and beyond it a busy street. But which street? By standing as high as she could, she caught a glimpse of china-blue sea to her right, a dark peninsula of land with something battlemented like a toy fort built on the end. Bennelong Point, could that be it? But the street itself drew her gaze. Dirty, draggletail, it was nevertheless an important street, as she could see from the carriages and the jaunty horse-drawn sulkies that jolted past. The extraordinary thing was that the pedestrians seemed more important than the wheeled traffic.

Abigail, coming from a time where a pedestrian ventured onto the road at his peril, could scarcely believe it. The roadway itself was crowded with people crossing at all angles; filthy scamps of children played with a skipping rope; a man was driving a small herd of goats; there were street barrows laden with fish, old clothes, boots, garbage, and even a water barrel. A man passed at a fast trot. He wore a dozen hats, one on top of the other. A board about his neck proclaimed *Tanner Heach, Hatts All Clane.*

Abigail mumbled this over to herself and at last worked it out. She laughed.

'Do come and look, Gibbie. It's fun!'

But the boy was bawling: 'She's gunna open the window and kill me! Dovey, Granny, Faither, she'll open the window if you dunna take care!'

Abigail had not thought of opening the window. Now she gave it a heave, but the sash was screwed down. She withdrew her head, and became aware that there was uproar in the shop, Dovey and Granny scolding, a strange male voice, of a customer perhaps, raised in a yell of pain and fury. Mr Bow stormed into the parlour. Ignoring Abigail and the cowering Gibbie, he jerked down a rusty sword that hung by a green tasselled cord above the mantel.

'The Rooshians are coming, fousands of 'em! Let's show 'em what we're made of, lads! Hearts of oak, hearts of oak!' he roared as he charged out, and Abigail hopped to the window just in time to see him pelting down the street, the people scattering before him.

'Wow!' cried Abigail. She went into the shop.

Dovey was pale and frightened. 'I dunna ken how he got at the rum, Granny, honest! He must have had it hid. And he's spilt all the glessie, just as it was about to crackle, and scattered the lemon bonbons everywhere!'

Abigail saw also that Dovey's arm was streaked with a

69

long burn; but the girl said nothing about it, so neither did Abigail. She understood the situation now. Mr Bow was a placid, timid man until he drank, and then his head filled with fancies and he ran wild.

Mrs Tallisker was taking off her apron. Her firm brown face was calm but stern, her lips compressed.

'I'll be awa' after him, lass. You try to make order here.'

She took Dovey's stick, which was leaning against the wall, and marched out. She took no notice whatsoever of the soldier, treacle-plastered from top to toe, swearing without pause for breath.

Abigail limped over to him. 'You!' she commanded. 'Shut up!'

He ceased in mid-expletive, and snarled, 'I'll get ten days in the clink for having me gear in this state. The sergeant will say I'm a slummerkin and very likely sozzled.'

'And so you are,' said Abigail boldly. 'You stink like a barrel of beer. Tell your officer it was an accident.'

'And who are you, ordering one of the Queen's men around, you damned saucy wench? Sure, you're as homely as a cow's behind.'

'That may be,' replied Abigail, 'but there's one thing I'll tell you . . . get out of here before Mr Bow returns or he'll take you for a Russian and slice off your head like the pumpkin it is!'

The soldier backed out, but not before he shouted, 'They'll have Bow in Bedlam if he don't keep off the wet!'

'But he only drinks because of his sorrow, poor man,' said Dovey. 'And when he does he goes awa' out of his head. But it's true . . . sooner or later they'll come and put him away. Oh, if only Judah were home – he can manage him, and keep him from the drink, too!'

Abigail peeped out the door. There was a brief commotion down on the corner. She saw Granny's tall white bonnet bobbing above the crowd.

'Granny's got him,' Abigail called to Dovey, 'and there's two men with him holding his arms.'

'Oh, the Dear help us,' gasped Dovey. 'Not the constables?'

She, too, hurried down the street. Abigail, her ankle beginning to pain savagely, clung to the lintel of the door and looked eagerly and urgently about her. The shop was on a corner. Five stone steps, scooped out like ladles with wear, led to the footpath of slab timber sunk in the earth and interspersed with areas of cobbles and rough gravel. To her right was the Argyle Cut. She was amazed to see above it a rock precipice surmounted by excellent mansions. Late winter roses wavered over their massive stone walls. It seemed incredible that wealthy people lived up there, with all the stenches and rat-ridden poverty of The Rocks washing up to their back fences like a disgusting tide. But she had no time to ponder that now. Through the struts of the wooden bridge that spanned The Cut she saw the low peaked roof of the Garrison Church. *That* had not changed. Abigail's heart jumped with excitement. Now she knew where she was. The confectionery shop was on the corner of Cambridge and Argyle streets. To the right was Circular Quay, and George Street, and between them and Mr Bow's shop was Harrington Street, where she had first accidentally stumbled into the nineteenth century.

Looking down there now she caught glimpses of the Harbour, and saw Granny's tall form and white cap, and Mr Bow himself, sagging between a mighty blue-aproned butcher in a bowler hat and a floury-faced baker in a stiff white paper crown. All the fire had gone out of Mr Bow.

Abigail trembled with relief and joy. As far as time went she might be a long way from home, but in space she was just five minutes from the alley up which she had come from Mitchell and the children's playground.

'I don't need Beatie's help after all,' she thought. 'The poor kid hated promising to do it, anyway, going against her granny and everything. But I'll have to wait till my ankle is a little better, and this bruise gone from my face. I can't let poor Mum see that – she'll be frantic enough as it is. I'll just have to bide my time, that's all, and climb out a window if necessary.'

Dovey and Granny gently lowered the collapsed form of Mr Bow to a bench in the shop.

The butcher, who had the rusty old sword over his shoulder, said gruffly, 'You ought to throw this old pig-sticker away, Missus. Only brings back memories to the poor silly cove. Better forgotten, I say, wars and all them things. Well, Barney 'n me'll leave you, me old cock-sparrer. Back you go to the gobstoppers.'

Dovey hastily closed the door behind them and barred it. The little shop was an indescribable mess: treacle and half-solidified caramel all over the floor; the piles of shining tins cast down; the huge cauldrons that hung over the fire sullenly spitting and glugging.

'I'll help,' said Abigail. 'Give me an apron.'

While Granny stirred the cauldrons and blew up the fire to redness again, Abby got down on the floor with a brush and bucket and scraped up the sugary mess. Mr Bow, as though in a trance, sat yellowish and silent. He smelled strongly of rum.

Gibbie trailed out from the parlour, saying pathetically, 'I'm a very sick laddie, and there's not one of you has been to see if I'm quick or dead.'

'You go up to bed, if you're poorly,' said Dovey soothingly. She passed a hand over the little boy's forehead. 'There, you're no' so hot today. Why, you're a deal better!'

'Nay, nay,' said Gibbie crossly, 'I'm no' fit to climb all those stairs. I'll wait till I'm carried.'

As he trailed back into the parlour Abigail thought, 'Little fake! Making the most of it.'

Scrubbing away, she found opportunity to look closely at the shop. The walls were whitewashed, and the surrounds of the vast open fireplace made crimson with a glossy paste. The grates, the spits and hooks, were bright. Only the outside of the four large cauldrons, dangling from their hooks and chains, were sooted over. On the wall, over an iron hook, hung a solidified cascade of toffee that Dovey had been pulling to make it creamy and malleable.

'It's ruined, I fear,' Dovey said gloomily. 'That's Black Man, Abby. 'Tis cut into six-inch sticks with scissors. What a sad loss of good treacle.'

'Not so, hen,' said Mrs Tallisker. She lifted the huge irregular slab of toffee onto a marble work bench, gave it a whack with a little mallet. It shattered into hundreds of pieces of glassy amber.

'Put it in the big trencher, lass, and into the window with it. We'll sell it at a ha'penny the quarter.'

The windows were not display windows but cottage windows of many-paned glass, with benches behind them where the wares could be shown. When the girls had cleaned the floor and washed themselves, Dovey showed Abigail the many different sweets Mr Bow could concoct. Gundy, flavoured with cinnamon or aniseed; fig and almond cake, which was a lemon-flavoured toffee poured over pounded fruit or nuts and allowed to set; Peggy's Leg; liquorice; and the favourite glessie, a kind of honeycomb. Abigail had never seen any of these sweets before, but did not say so.

73

At last everything was spotless again. Gibbie appeared from the parlour and gazed reproachfully at them all.

'And what about poor wee Gibbie?' he inquired.

'Oh, Gibbie love,' pleaded Dovey, 'we must wait for Beatie to come from school to help Granny carry you up. Ye ken verra weel I'm no use at all, and Abby can scarce walk.'

'Me faither is offending Providence by touching the speerits,' pronounced Gibbie, stern as a parson. 'He canna even carry his wee dying laddie up to his bed!'

As though on cue, Mr Bow produced a great roaring sob, dropped his head in his hands and wept bitterly. 'My 'Melia, my 'Melia, how will I raise the young 'uns without you? Why did you go for to leave me, wife?'

'Because God called her, Samuel,' said Granny gently. 'Would you go against His holy will?'

Gibbie began to croak and grunt about the soreness of his throat, the feebleness of his legs, and Abigail gave him a sharp nip on the back of the neck. He yelped once and shot up the stairs roaring. Dovey limped after him.

'That was not kind, Abigail,' said Granny, with the nearest thing to severity the girl had yet heard in the old woman's beautiful voice.

'Maybe not,' said Abigail, 'but it worked, didn't it? That youngster will turn into an invalid and get his four black horses and his wee white coffin if he's not pushed out into the fresh air and sunshine. If Beatie can recover from the fever and go back to her lessons, why can't he?'

'Ah,' said the old woman with a sigh. 'Beatie is different. She has a will like iron. The Dear alone knows what will become of her, with all the wild thoughts she has. But there, hen, you should be resting that ankle. I'll just get Mr Bow to bed, and then I'll put a wee poultice on it for you.'

The poultice was of mashed and heated comfrey leaves, which Mrs Tallisker called 'boneset'. A comfrey paste was also applied to the bruise on the girl's face. It must have been effective, for day by day the bruise faded.

Now that she felt confident of making her escape when she was fit enough, Abigail began to observe the Bows and Talliskers more closely than she had previously done.

When she had first come to this time she had been like a plane passenger who had disembarked in the wrong country, without luggage or passport. But now she knew where she was. She knew that she could leave.

She realised there would be many problems. Her parents would be half crazy with anxiety; they would certainly have alerted the police. She had no idea what she could tell them back in her own time. No one would believe her.

There was also the problem of clothes. Dovey's blouse and skirt, so heavy, so much the wrong shape and the wrong length, the frightful stockings that made even Abigail's slim legs look like striped woollen table legs – how could she explain them? Even in a Sydney where almost everyone dressed casually Dovey's clothes were so uncouth they could not possibly be anyone's choice.

'Well,' thought Abigail, 'I'll meet those hassles when I come to them. First I have to be able to walk properly on this ankle and, if possible, have a face that doesn't look as if it's been caught in a door.'

She began to look attentively at these people amongst who she had come to live. After all, she thought, there aren't many twentieth-century girls who can speak of Victorian times from experience.

The first thing was their kindness. How amazingly widespread it was ... the butcher and the baker catching and bringing back Mr Bow in his frenzy; even the treacle-smeared soldier, who she was sure would not blame the confectioner for his accident. And then, herself. Suppose some strange girl had been knocked down outside Magpies, what would her own mother have done? Brought her inside, rung the ambulance, sent her flowers in hospital, perhaps worried a little whether Magpies' insurance covered such accidents. And yet Kathy Kirk was the most soft-hearted of women. But here were these people, not as poor as some of the malformed scarecrows that dawdled around the lanes perhaps, but still far from comfortably settled; people, too, who had recently suffered a painful bereavement: And yet they had believed her worse off than they were, a solitary girl with only the clothes she stood up in. They had taken responsibility for her, nursed and clothed her. Someone had given up her bed, probably Beatie; no one had complained when she was snappish and rude about Dovey's best clothes, about the lack of sanitation; no one had condemned her unsympathetic attitude towards Gibbie.

'I'm not kind,' said Abigail with a sickish surprise. 'Look how I went on with Mum when she said she wanted us to get together with Dad again. Look what I did to Dad when I was little, punched him on the nose and made it bleed. Maybe I've never been really kind in my life.'

And she remembered with a pang what Kathy had said, that awful day: that she had never, either as a child or a fourteen-year-old, offered a word of sympathy to her mother.

'Yet here are these people, happy and grateful to be able to read and write, just to be allowed to earn a living; and they've shared everything they can share with me, whom they don't know from Adam.'

These Victorians lived in a dangerous world, where a whole family could be wiped out with typhoid fever or smallpox, where a soldier could get a hole in his head that you could put your fist in, where there were no pensions or free hospitals or penicillin or proper education for girls, or even poor boys, probably. Yet, in a way, it was a more human world than the one Abigail called her own.

'I wish I could stay awhile,' she thought, 'and find out why all these things are. But I can't think about any of this till I get home. Getting home, that's what I have to plan.'

# Chapter 6

The day Abigail ran away to go home started like any other day. As usual she was wearing clothes borrowed from Dovey, flannel underwear and a brown gingham dress covered by a long white pinafore. She felt draggy and looked it.

She had noted that the ladies in the carriages dashing through to Kent and Cumberland streets – some of them being real ladies and others, according to the cynical Beatie, only 'high-steppers', or women unacceptable to polite society – wore lace jabots, handsome buttons and silk braids, and tight jackets that narrowed to fish tails at the rear.

Working women wore drab, ankle-length dresses with long sleeves and aprons. And whereas the rich ladies and the dashing high-steppers both peacocked in saucer-shaped hats tipped forward to make room for elaborate chignons of plaits and curls, the working women flung shawls over their centre-parted, smoothly brushed, or, more often, disorderly and dusty, hair.

It was hard to tell a high-stepper from a real lady, thought Abigail; but you would never mistake one or the other for a working-class woman. She understood now why Kathy never got any lower-class Victorian clothing at Magpies. It had all been worn out by unceasing labour a hundred years before.

'Mum knows a lot about Victorian and Edwardian

78

days,' ruminated Abigail, 'but she has no idea how hard the women worked!'

'Are the high-steppers prostitutes?' Abigail innocently asked Dovey.

Dovey flushed 'Oh, Abby, never let Granny hear you use such language! It'd fair make her swoon awa'.'

Abby added prostitutes to the list of things she was not to mention: the Deity, legs (in front of menfolk), any natural function (except in whispers), the privy at the end of the yard, which consisted of a can and a scrubbed wooden seat (this was 'the wee hoosie').

'Lot of blanky rubbish,' said the outspoken Beatie when she was alone with Abigail, 'with The Rocks the way it is, full of seamen and soldiers and language to curl your hair. Not to mind some of the worst grog shops and crimp houses in Sydney.'

'What's a crimp house?' asked Abigail.

'A grog shop where they put opium in the seamen's drink, and then shanghai them away to ships that need crews and can't get them, leaky old tubs bound for China and maybe intended to sink so that the owners will get the insurance. So Judah says.'

'But that's cold-blooded murder,' cried Abigail. 'Things like that can't go on in these days!'

'Do they no' go on in yours?' asked Beatie hopefully.

'I don't think so,' said Abigail.

She could not bring herself to tell the eager Beatie about nuclear bombs, chemical warfare, napalm bombing of peasants' villages and fields. The little girl thought of the late twentieth century as a sort of paradise, a place of marvels. In some ways it was a paradise compared with Beatie's own time. Let her go on believing there was no dark side, thought Abigail. She would not live to see it, anyway.

On the day Abigail tried to run away to her own time

she was not wearing Mrs Tallisker's best buttoned boots, though now her ankle was its normal size again. Granny had bought her second-hand shoes from the boot barrow. They were heel-less slippers of kid, very uncomfortable, and the barrow man had passed cheeky remarks about the size of her feet. That was another thing she hadn't known: that even Victorian working women had tiny feet.

Beatie went off to the Ragged School. She was excited because Judah's ship was in port; he would be home that night.

'And I've learnt how to decline six Latin verbs,' she told Abigail joyfully. 'Judah teaches me.'

'Has Judah studied Latin, then?'

'Oh, aye, has he not!' said Beatie proudly. 'And wasn't he top of the class when he was only thirteen. Mr Taylor gave him a grand book, *Travels in Africa*, with "First Prize for Scholarship" and his name written in copperplate, and he sorely wanted him to go to Fort Street School for Boys; but Judah, he was that set on the sea and he wunna!'

'Who's Mr Taylor?' asked Abigail.

'Oh, he's the headmaster of Trinity Parish School, y'ken, and he took Judah into his special class for promising boys. Aye, promising, that's what he said about our Judah. Smart as a whip he is, and will be master of his own vessel some day.'

Mr Bow had been very morose and silent since his last escapade; he was a wretched man, and Abigail was sorry for him. It must have been a terrible thing to lose his wife and little son all in a day. This child was not the only one he and Amelia Bow had lost. Three daughters had died of the smallpox. They had come between Judah and Beatie. Judah had taken the disease too, but lightly. The pock on his cheek, that looked like a dimple, was the only sign of it.

Abigail had not looked closely at Judah's face: she had been too frightened and confused that night. But she remembered the quaint way he had got her name out of her, and the ease with which he had lifted her to look out the window – to find that her own world had vanished as if by enchantment. She tried to get Mr Bow to talk about his children, but he only gave her a piteous look from those preposterously crossed eyes, and she desisted.

She was making bonbons for Granny. They were small squares of orange and lemon peel threaded on a fine steel knitting-needle. Abigail dipped the needle into a pot of boiling sugar flavoured with grated lemon and a drop of purest whale-oil.

'To keep the syrup from brittling,' explained Granny. These bonbons were then laid carefully on a buttered slab of marble and allowed to get cold and crisp before they were packed in paper cones for sale.

It was interesting, thought Abigail, how she had been so absorbed into The Rocks area without further question. The fiction that she was an immigrant girl of good education and no kin, bound for a situation on the High Rocks, knocked down and injured by Mr Bow in one of his spells, and now without memory or worldly resources, had been accepted by those customers made curious by her occasional presence in the shop. She had now been two weeks with the Bows, and there had been no further reference to that curious conversation between Granny and Dovey about her lost green dress. Nor would Beatie answer any questions about 'the Stranger'. She shut her mouth like a rat-trap and admitted frankly: 'I'm that scared of Granny. She'd murder me if she knew what I've told ye already. She's got the power, I've told ye over and over again!'

'You're dotty!' said Abigail. 'Granny would never hurt

you, or anyone else. She's the best soul in the world.'

''Tisn't that she'd hurt me,' explained Beatie reluctantly. 'But she'd look at me. And I dinna want Granny to look at me.'

And that was all she would say.

Yet Beatie was relentless in her questioning of Abigail about the years to come. Abigail told her about jet aircraft, about men landing on the moon and their voices and pictures coming all the way to earth, clear and bright. She told her about new countries that did not exist in Beatie's day.

'But where is the Empire?' Beatie asked, baffled.

Abigail did not know. 'It just seemed to break up and dribble away,' she admitted lamely.

'But who's looking after the black men?'

'They're looking after themselves,' said Abigail. But Beatie could not understand. 'Black men canna look after themselves. Don't be daft!'

Abigail was constantly surprised at what Beatie would believe and what she could not accept for a second. That men could land on the moon, yes. That people bathed naked from public beaches, no. She scoffed at the idea that there were only three or four kings and queens left in the world, but believed without question that many married folk divorced and married others.

'For rich folk do the same right now,' she said in her matter-of-fact way. 'But for a housewifie now, should her man starve or beat her and the bairns, there's naught but running away or rat poison.'

Most of all she wanted to know about people, whether girls could become doctors, teachers, do good and useful things. Abigail was glad to be able to say 'yes'.

Always these conversations ended the same way.

'But how did those bairnies know my name? Dinna ye ha' some more ideas, Abby? I tell ye, I'm ettlin' to find out, come what may!'

The older children at the Ragged School had their lessons after dinner-time whistle, a midday orchestra of hideous noises from steam cranes, factories, and loading ships. It was taken for granted by the Ragged School board that the children worked for a living. Some were boot blacks or newspaper boys in the city; others ran errands for offices, or delivered for merchants; many were 'sparrow-starvers' or sweepers of manure. Each youngster did something, anything, to earn a few pennies, and many of their parents resented their wasting afternoons at the Ragged School.

On this fateful afternoon, Beatie had long gone off, grizzling and fiery-eyed over the 'lassies' rubbish' she would be taught. Granny and Dovey were upstairs with Gibbie; Mr Bow, hoop-backed, speechless and glum, stirred a cauldron, his back to Abigail.

Abigail delicately placed the last skewer of bonbons to dry on the marble slab, and walked without haste out of the shop.

It was late in the afternoon. The ships' masts, bare as trees after a bushfire, stood up in the Harbour, very straight, like a thousand spillikins, criss-crossed and twigged with spars and lesser gear. The westering sun seized upon bright specks of metal on these masts and made them burn like stars. Abigail walked straight down Argyle Street.

Not for a moment did it occur to her that she was not going home, to her mother, her father, the bear chair, Magpies, school. All she had to do was turn up Harrington Street, find the stairway and the lane up which she and

Beatie had run, and she would descend towards George Street and Circular Quay, and see Mitchell standing there in its steel and glassy grandeur.

'My father designed it,' she had told Beatie, who looked at her as if she were lying.

There were trees in Argyle Street, oaks, she thought, covered with curdy green. Many alleys spindled away, turning into flights of steps as steep as ships' companionways as they went up and over looming sandstone knobs and reefs. Sometimes houses perched on these outcrops like beached Arks; sometimes they were built into them so that the back wall of the house was living sandstone. The lanes were runnels of wet and filth between mouldering shops, factories and cottages. The whole place was cankered with poverty and neglect. The people also – all had something the matter with them: rotting teeth, clubfeet, a cheek puckered by a burn. A little girl, dressed fantastically in a woman's trailing dress and squashed hat, snarled, 'Ooya starin' at?' and raised a dirty fist as if to strike. Abigail saw that the little one's face was despoiled by a hare-lip.

But who could fix these infirmities in Victorian days? wondered Abigail. If you were born crooked, you stayed crooked and made the best of it, as Granny Tallisker made the best of the violent deprivation of her son Robert, her daughter Amelia, the four grandchildren dead before they grew up. It was all God's will.

The gutters, made of two tipped stones, were full of garbage. Abigail saw scaly tails twitching amongst the rotting debris and sprang away.

'Steady on, Missie!' It was an elderly soldier with a roast-beef face. He held his musket horizontally so that she could not pass, and she saw a gang of convicts clanking across the street. Some had yellow jackets with large letters and figures daubed in black and red. Others wore coarse canvas cover-alls, part grey, part brown, like grotesque harlequins. Those who were chained had hitched up their chains to their belts with fragments of rope or rag, so that they could walk. But their walk was a slow, bandy-legged shuffle.

She said, 'I thought transportation stopped years and years ago!'

'These canaries are long-termers, Miss. They bin loading coal down yonder.'

'It's terrible, terrible,' she whispered.

The soldier said with harsh kindness, 'You just out from the Old Country, Miss? Well, New South Wales ain't no place of harps and angels, that's sartin.'

He stiffened to attention. Abigail saw a young officer, very dandified and bored, ride out from under one of the flattened arches that marked the many courts or wynds. He cut carelessly with his crop at the mob of skeleton, matted-hair urchins that milled about his horse, yelping, 'Chuck us down a copper, Guv!' and rode after the convicts.

Now she was outside the Ragged School. She passed it cautiously, for she did not want to meet Beatie unexpectedly. She heard from within the drone of many voices reciting the Lord's Prayer, the sudden whip-like whistle of a willow cane. But even as she sighed for the pauper children within, she heard behind her the hoarse voice of Beatie Bow.

'Eh, it's Abigail! Abby, come back! Where are ye off to?'

Abigail plunged across the street. A stunted child, face black with a lifetime's dirt, ceased sweeping horse manure and whacked at her legs with his broom so that she almost fell. Her first thought was that Beatie had called from one of the school windows, but now she saw her, accompanied by the sturdy figure of Judah, running along from the direction of the wharves.

It had not occurred to her that Beatie would play truant from school to go to meet her brother. But there they were, dodging amongst the crowd, gaining on her every minute.

She could not see the lamp-post that marked the stairs she had ascended on that first night; it was too late to look for the right alley. So she dived into the first opening she noticed. It was so narrow she could have spanned it with her arms. Its uneven cobbles ran sluggishly with thick green slime. Pressed against the wall, she saw Beatie and Judah run past.

Suddenly a hand fastened round her ankle. She looked down and saw a frightful thing grinning gap-toothed at her. It was a legless man, on a little low trolley like a child's push-cart. He had a big bulging forehead and fingers as sinuous as steel.

'Let me go!' panted Abigail. With her free foot she kicked at the man's face, but he dodged her with the nimbleness of a monkey. Laughing, he dragged her closer, and bit her leg just above the ankle. The pain was bad enough, but the horror that seized the girl was unbearable.

She let out a ringing shriek. 'Beatie, Judah, help, help!'

That was all she could utter, for a bag smelling of rotten fish descended over her head and was pulled tight. She was half carried, half dragged she knew not where. Abigail was a strong girl, and her hands were free. She hammered and punched, scratched and tore. Once her fingers fastened in a beard: she could tell by the bristly texture of it. She gave a great yank and a handful came out. The owner slapped her repeatedly over the ears, cursing in an accent and tones such as she had never heard.

'You've caught yourself no tame puss-cat there, Hannah!' a husky voice said with a chuckle. Abigail's hands were deftly snared and tied behind her back, and the sack was whisked off her head. She was in a dark, evil-smelling room, and before her stood a mountainous woman holding a blood-spattered fist to her hairy chin. She must have weighed nearly a hundred kilos; there seemed no end to her in her full skirts and vast blouse of gaudy striped silk. Out of the sleeves poked sausagey hands covered in rings. Ferret eyes gleamed at Abigail; the sausage hands filled themselves with her hair and jerked brutally.

'I'll have yer bald!' she yelled. Abigail shrieked at the full power of her lungs, and kicked violently at everything she could see or reach.

A hand went over her mouth. It was accustomed to holding captives thus, for it pushed her upper lip down over her teeth so that she could not bite.

'Hold on now, Hannah,' said the husky voice. 'We've a pretty little canary bird here; she'll go for a sweet sum, fifteen quid or more. But not if you take off all her hair at the roots.'

Abigail glared over the hand at the bearded woman. She had never seen anything so grotesque in her life. Whether the creature had come from a circus or not, she was terrifying.

Yet, now that the first shock was over, Abigail felt mad fury rather than panic. The panic ran underneath the anger, like a fast-rising tide. She realised clearly that she was in the kind of peril of which she had never dreamed. For the room contained many people, and there was no way, even if she could get her hands free, that she could fight her way out.

The room was, she thought, an underground kitchen.

It was like a lair or cavern, pitch black except for a few candle stubs stuck in bottles or their own grease, and the murky gleam of a vast open fireplace. The smell was terrible, even for The Rocks – not only of unwashed and crowded humanity, but decayed meat and rotting wood.

A girl in a draggletail pink wrapper wandered over and looked at her curiously. She seemed half imbecile, with no front teeth and a nose with a flattened bridge. Picking this nose industriously, she lisped, 'She ain't much to look at, Master. Be she right age, you think? Mebbe with her 'air frizzed out and some paint on she'd pass in twilight.'

Abigail felt her skin creep.

'Shut your trap, Effie,' said the husky voice. 'She's fresh as a new-laid egg. What else matters?'

Abigail felt a hand stealing around the hem of her skirt. Twisting sideways, she saw the terrible little cripple sniffing about her ankles like a dog.

'She taste sweet as a newborn mouse, Hannah,' he cajoled. 'Let poor Barker have a nibble.'

'Sho, you cannibal,' shouted the woman. 'Mark her and I'll do fer yer, I swear I will.'

The husky voice now said, almost with kindness, 'Just out from the Old Country, are you, my pet?'

Abigail nodded.

'Hannah will see you right,' went on the voice. 'Heart of gold, Hannah, though it's a long way in, eh, Hannah?'

The fat woman snarled. But it was plain she was afraid of the man with the husky voice. He now said, 'If I take away my hand, will you be quiet, like the dear child you are?'

Abigail nodded, and the hand was removed from her mouth. Instantly she yelled, 'Ju . . .' But she got no further. A kerchief was thrust between her teeth and tied behind her head, and she was given a push that sent her sprawling into a corner. She was now able to see that the owner of the husky voice was a handsome man, a gentleman, as Beatie would have said, in well-fitted breeches, a tailored coat of cocoa colour, and a dashing tall beaver to match.

He held a tiny bouquet of jonquils and fern to his nose, presumably to keep the smells away.

'She's to be kept close,' he instructed the bearded woman, jerking his head at the ceiling. He took out a gold watch, sprang open its lid, and shut it again. He said, 'In the morning, Hannah, and I don't want the goods damaged.' Without another look at Abigail he strolled out.

Now Abigail began to sweat with growing terror. If Judah and Beatie had not seen her duck into the little alley, what chance would she have? The bearded woman came over, a rag still held to her bloody chin, and said venomously, 'Lucky for you the master took a fancy to yer. But don't think I ain't able to hurt you bad where it don't show.'

Abigail swallowed with difficulty. Her mouth was dry. The scarf was salty with dirt and sweat. She retched a little. She thought desperately, 'I can't lose my head, whatever I do.'

She made herself breathe quietly. But something soft and squashy moved beneath her. She realised with horror that it was a woman, a kind of woman, for shortly it wriggled feebly out from underneath her and showed itself in the candlelight to be a hobgoblin with tangled hay-like hair, cheeks bonfire red with either rouge or fever, and a body hung with parti-coloured rags.

She crept over to the table, and began to tear at a

mildewed crust of bread. One of the other women, wearing a flounced red petticoat and a black corset and little else, good-naturedly pushed over to the wreck an anonymous hunk of meat that might have been a rooster's neck.

'Here, Doll,' she said. 'Don't eat that muck you got there. Ruin your gut it will.'

The wreck stuffed it in her mouth, bone and all, but before she did she said in a voice of extreme refinement, 'Thank you, Sarah, I'm much obliged.'

'Oh, God,' thought Abigail, 'that thing has had an education. It might even have been a *lady*.'

Now she was paralysed with terror. She could imagine herself as another Doll in twenty years' time, all spirit beaten out of her, sodden with booze and disease, not even fit for the life of degradation the gentleman with the husky voice evidently intended for her. No matter how fiercely she blinked, tears filled her eyes and fell down on the gag.

One of the other girls strolled over to her. She was fancily dressed, with much flouncing and many ribbons, and a large hat with a purple ostrich feather. Below this hat was a young plump face, pretty and good-natured. Abigail noticed that she, like Dovey, uncannily resembled a Victorian doll.

'It must be their idea of good looks,' thought Abigail hazily. 'No wonder everyone's always telling me how homely I am.'

The girl smiled, showing chalky teeth. 'Don't pipe your eye, duck; 'tisn't such a bad old life. Better than starving on slop work in the factories, any old how. I'm the dress-lodger, and me name's Em'ly, but I call meself Maude 'cos it's more posh. Come on, Doll, the lamps is lit, time we was getting on the road.'

All of this, spoken in a thick south London accent, was

scarcely comprehensible to Abigail. But she was to find out that the handsomest girl in the house was called the dress-lodger, sent out in garments belonging to the proprietor, always with an attendant to see that she didn't run off with them.

But Doll began to cough and splutter. Her eyes rolled up; she looked as if she were going to die.

'Gawd, I'm not going off with that death's head trailing behind me,' protested Maude. 'It'd scare off Robinson Crusoe.'

So another famine-wasted object was dragged out of a corner, arrayed respectably, and pushed forward to follow Maude. Maude protested, but finally laughed and set off.

Doll cringed timidly as Hannah stood over her.

'You good-for-nothing, you scarecrow! You're fit for the bone-yard, that's all, breathing pestilence over us all.'

'Chuck her out, Hannah,' advised one of the men who sat smoking a cutty pipe by the fire. They seemed to have nothing to do with the establishment as customers or protectors. Abigail guessed that they were employed by the gentleman proprietor to bully the women's takings from them and keep an eye on Hannah's honesty.

'Ah, well,' said Hannah, putting on a ludicrous face of long-suffering virtue, 'if I ain't charitable towards me own niece I dunno what the rest of you villains can expect. Here, you, Chow, take the new 'un up to the attic, and you come up and keep an eye on her, Doll.'

Chow, an emaciated half-Asian, seized Abigail as though she weighed no more than a cat, carried her up stairs built of rough-hewn baulks of timber, and at last dropped her on a sagging pallet. Doll sidled breathlessly about Hannah, beseeching, 'Just a little gin, Aunt dear. Twopenceworth would be sufficient. Just enough to keep my cough from annoying our guest.'

'Here y'are, then, and don't say I ain't a good aunt to you, bit o' useless rubbish that you are.'

Hannah dug into a depthless pocket and fished up a small bottle. Doll seized it with tearful gratitude. Hannah cautioned her to keep a keen eye on Abigail.

'Them rats are partial to a nice bit o' fresh chicken,' she said. Abigail could hear rats scampering over the ceiling. Hannah saw her look upwards and grinned, satisfied.

'They come out in their fousands.' She chuckled. Placing the candlestick on a box in the corner, she jerked her head at Chow. The door slammed, and Abigail heard a key turn and a bar clank home.

She wanted to cry but she knew that if she did she would choke on the gag. To distract herself she looked around at the attic. Doll, lying on a sack beside the pallet, sucked luxuriously at her bottle.

The attic did not have the proportions or the sloping roof of the usual attic, such as the one Gibbie slept in. The window, too, was almost as large as a door. And then, those stairs . . . they were not stairs anyone would build in a house. Abby tried to think as sensibly as she could.

Was it likely that houses, however derelict, would stand beside such a narrow alley? The walls of the attic seemed to be made of blocks of bare stone. That, too, was uncommon. There was no fireplace and, as she had now learnt from Beatie, almost every room in every house in Sydney, no matter how poor, had a fireplace.

She realised with despair that she was too frightened to make sense of it. Her thoughts began to chase one another round and round.

'Like those rats up there,' she thought. Sometimes her whole body shuddered spasmodically, as if she were lying on an ice floe. She was aware in the direst way of her great

92

danger. It could be that she would never be seen again in 1873, let alone her own time. She had nothing to hope for except that Judah and Beatie had heard the first great yell she had given.

She forced herself to lie quiet. There was no one to help her, no one at all. But she could not give up without a battle. Whatever she could do to escape, she had to try to do.

She had an imaginative flash of her grandmother, addressing her perm in resigned tones: 'She's dodgy, Katherine. Not one of your nice frank open-faced girls. You're too soft and protective. Heaven help her if she ever has to fend for herself.'

'We'll see about that, you old bat,' thought Abigail. But her bravado was false. If her grandmother had come through the door, smiling her bogus smile, Abigail would have welcomed her like an angel.

But Grandmother would never come through the door. Grandmother had not yet been born.

Abigail, with one eye on Doll, began to strain at the fabric that bound her hands. It seemed to be another kerchief. She twisted it patiently, at last got a thumb free and, after half an hour, the fingers of one hand.

Doll drank, sometimes wept, the tears oozing like oil out of the black-socketed eyes. She mumbled and sang, sometimes seemed to speak to her companion, though perhaps it was to herself.

'My name is Dorothea Victoria Brand. I had God-fearing parents. Mother was ill-educated, like Aunt Hannah, and Father married beneath him. He was a clerk in a counting house. He saw that I went to school, a boarding-school on the moors. It was very cold there, but I was happy. I was a bookish child. Clever and industrious, that's what the Board said. Father wanted me to have private tutoring in French and singing, but he could not afford it. He wept, I remember. He loved me dearly, did my father.'

It's a warehouse or bond store, that's what it is, thought Abigail suddenly. A disused one. And that window might be the kind that opens on a platform, with a pulley and rope for hauling up bags of flour and stuff.

She got the other hand out, and with infinite slowness untied the gag at the back of her head. She clamped the gag between her teeth, did not shift her position, and kept her gaze on Doll.

'Father was taken suddenly. His horse rolled on him. And Mother went labouring in a slop-shop, making sailors' smocks. Twenty girls in a room ten by ten – think of it! – stitch, stitch, fourteen hours a day without a breath of fresh air. So Mother took the lung fever. Thirty-two she was when God took her. So the parish Board sent me out to Mother's sister. I had my thirteenth birthday on the ship *Corona*. That was ten long years ago.'

Abigail froze. Could this tottering ruin of a woman be only twenty-three? Doll pushed herself half upright, fell into a fearful paroxysm of coughing, and subsided once more. Her breath rattled in her chest in a frightening way; she seemed in a stupor.

'Aunt Hannah,' she whispered hoarsely, 'she put me to work. I didn't starve, you know.'

Abigail slipped to her feet. There was an iron bar across the two shutters that formed the window. It took her a long time to work it out of its rusted sockets. As she tried to open the shutter, it squawked alarmingly. Doll opened one glazed eye, but seemed not to have the strength to open the other. A trickle of bloodstained dribble came from her mouth.

'A person will do many things rather than starve,' she

murmured. 'That's what the parsons don't understand. Empty bellies speak louder than the Ten Commandments.'

She closed her eyes again. In the uncertain light her face was that of a skull.

Abigail was frightened out of her wits. 'Mum!' she thought. 'I want you, Mum!' She wanted to pray but couldn't think of any words, so instead she put forth all her strength and shouted silently, 'Granny! Help me, help me!'

But it was to Granny Tallisker and not her own grandmother that her thoughts had turned. The shutter moved, and opened, and a gush of damp, kerosene-laden air came into the room. A glaring yellow light, broken by dancing shadows, fanned up from the little court below.

She had guessed right. There was a small wooden platform, supported on struts grown rotten and flimsy, in front of the window, and above it projected a rusty pulley and a frayed rope. She closed the shutter behind her, in case the cold air awakened Doll from her drunken slumber, and crouched on the platform. It groaned and dipped under her weight.

Nervously she gazed over the edge. Dark, shapeless things like bears or trolls gyrated about a brazier; coarse braying music from a tin whistle and a paper-covered comb filtered upwards. She could see above the lower roofs the gaslights of George Street, and she heard the chunk-splosh of the Manly ferry's paddlewheels as it left the Quay.

She saw now that the thread-like alleyway into which she had ducked to hide from Beatie and Judah led from Harrington Street to George Street. Half-way down this wretched short-cut was a yard upon which opened the back doors of two taverns. It was plain that they catered for the violent and degraded. A ragged thing flung out of a tavern door, to lie unconscious on the cobbles, had a face that might have belonged to a bulldog. The ruffians gyrating drunkenly around the brazier instantly fell upon this victim, and in a few moments it was naked. Abigail watched, paralysed with horror.

The platform creaked and shuddered. She could climb neither down nor up, unless the rope and pulley were usable. Some time towards morning, surely, the revellers below would be either asleep or dead drunk, and she could let herself down into the courtyard?

After a while she thought of testing the dangling rope. Cautiously she rose on tiptoe and seized it. The frayed ends fell almost into dust in her hand. The rope had not been used for years and was completely perished.

Her eyes filled with tears. There was no hope. As she stood there, looking up at the askew, rusted pulley, and the edge of the roof above it, a small patch of the sky suddenly lost its stars.

Someone was lying on the warehouse roof looking down at her.

# Chapter 7

When Abigail realised that she was being spied upon, her first horrified impulse was to get back into the room with Doll and bar the shutters. Her hand was on the pin when a voice said, very hushed, 'Dunna be feared, lass – it's me, Judah.'

She could see nothing but the shape of a head. She stood very still.

'Aye, that's bonny,' said the voice. 'That contraption ye're standing on might go any moment. Now, d'ye hear me all right?'

'Yes,' she breathed.

'I've some of the lads from the ship wi' me. I'm droppin' you a line with a loop in it. Put your foot in the loop and hold tight wi' all your might.'

A rope tumbled down to her. She seized it, did as she had been told, and whispered, 'I'm ready.'

As her chin rose above the roof slates, sturdy arms reached down and caught her under the armpits. In a few moments she was lying, limp and sweating, on the dewy slates.

There were several boys, two of them as small as Beatie, on the roof. They had bent the line around the stump of a chimney, and were now swiftly untying and coiling the rope. Barefooted and silent, they moved with the monkey-like nimbleness of apprentice seamen.

'How did you know where I was?' she asked.

'It was Granny,' said Judah, matter-of-factly. 'Go ahead, lads, and take care, for the roof's as rotten as them that own it.'

Keeping low, for fear anyone should see them outlined against the sky, Abigail and the boys crawled to the edge of the warehouse roof, and down the steep slippery gable of the terrace house next to it. If Abigail had not been so numbed with her recent experiences she would have been nervous of falling. But she had lost her shoes, and her stockinged toes, though not as deft as those of the boys, gripped fast in the mossy irregularities of the slates.

The boys pushed and pulled her across the roofs of six or seven little houses, sometimes disturbing rats playing in the guttering, or birds nesting in disused chimney-pots. She began to feel more and more unreal. Sometimes she thought she must have gone to sleep in the attic and was dreaming.

At last they came to a high rock lavishly curtained with convolvulus. A meagre lane squeezed between house and rock. Abigail cleared this space with ease.

'Why, she's as good as a lad!' said one of the boys. 'My sister Mabel would just 'a stood there squalling like a stood-on cat.'

Abigail, having slid down into the lane, was about to say that Mabel couldn't have been blamed when a curious thing happened. A wave of heat rippled up from her feet, leaving her legs boneless behind them.

She said feebly, 'I'm awfully sorry . . . my legs are gone somehow . . . and I think I might be sick . . .'

So she was, shivering and ashamed. But Judah merely said heartily, 'Chuck it up, Abby. It's a living wonder you're not in a dead swoon, what you've been through this night.'

She dimly heard the apprentice with the sister say, 'My sister Mabel would be flat on her back a'kicking and screeching in a fit of the flim-flams.'

'Poor old Mabel,' she tried to say, but nothing came out. Judah gathered her up, and she remembered no more until she realised she was being carried through the door of Mr Bow's shop. The other apprentices had vanished. She did not open her eyes again; it was too safe and comfortable against Judah's chest. If only, she felt drowsily, she could rest there for ever. But she had caught a glimpse of Dovey and Beatie, hovering about anxiously, and Gibbie in his long trailing night-shirt, flickering around like a small grey ghost, mad with curiosity.

Judah took her upstairs and laid her on her own bed. He said to Dovey, 'Granny?'

Dovey shook her head. 'Low.'

Abigail tried to speak, tried to ask, 'Is Granny Tallisker ill?' But although her mouth opened, her tongue moved, not a word came out. Terror filled her. What was the matter now? She caught Dovey's eye, pointed to her mouth, struggled to speak.

Dovey said soothingly, 'It's the shock, without doubt. Come the morning your voice will be back, as good as gold. Now then, so I can tell Granny when she's herself again: Did those villains do anything bad to you?'

Abigail longed to say, they kidnapped me and slapped me and a foul little beast with no legs bit me, and then they locked me up with a drunken consumptive who might be dead, as far as I know; but, no, they didn't do what I know you mean. But she could say nothing. She looked helplessly from Dovey to Judah and shook her head.

Judah said, 'I'll go take a keek at my granny, then.' He

came over to the bed, smoothed the tangled hair back from her forehead as if she were a child, and said, 'All's over now, Abby. Fret no more. Go to sleep and dream grand dreams, as you deserve.'

Abigail thought he had the most beautiful smile she had ever seen. The ruddy wholesomeness of his face contrasted so vividly with the fearful half-beast countenances of the inhabitants of the thieves' kitchen that she wanted to say, 'Thank you, thank you, Judah, for everything, not just for saving me. Thank you for being here.' But she could do nothing but press his hand.

He laughed, patted her cheek. 'You're a game lass, no doubt about that.'

Abigail still seemed to have no bones left in her body. Once again she was undressed by Dovey, given a posset, and put under the quilts. Dovey kissed her forehead, and hastened out.

Abigail thought, 'Mabel has the right idea. Lying on my back kicking and having hysterics is just what I'd do if I had any strength left.'

She became aware that Beatie was squatting on the end of the bed, like a malignant gnome. Abigail, already muzzy from the posset, had never seen her look so ferocious.

'What came over you, you blanky rattlebrain, to go down the Suez Canal? Could you not see it was the abode of cut-throats and mongrels? And what were you doing, fleein' away like that, when I'd given my solemn word to help you back to your ain time? Aye, and I wunna go back on it, neither, even though my poor granny is half dead on your account.'

'How, why?' Abigail wanted to ask. She managed a pitiful squawk.

'Never mind yer greeting, yer numbskull! Oh, couldn't I punch yer yeller and green!'

100

Abigail was only able to give a faint yelp of protest. She buried her face in the chicken-coop smelling pillow, and went unexpectedly to sleep. She awakened early, feeling stiff and sore all over. A faint daylight crept through the windows, early market carts grumbled over the cobbles. Dovey knelt beside her bed, her face in her hands.

'Oh, kind Lord in heaven, let my grandmother come to herself again, let poor Abby be as innocent as she was when she came to our care.'

Abigail managed a faint croak, and Dovey jumped up and came over to her. Abigail's voice still seemed to belong to someone else, but she whispered, 'Granny?'

'She's come back to herself, but she's no' well at all,' said Dovey evasively.

Abigail could not help it. Tears trickled down her cheeks.

'I'm just so tired of not understanding anything,' she said plaintively. 'It wouldn't matter if I weren't mixed up in it, but I am, and no one will tell me anything. It's not fair at all.'

Dovey looked both dubious and conscience-stricken. Across her childish face flitted a variety of expressions.

'Poor dear, poor child. 'Tis Granny herself who should tell you, as she meant to do. 'Twas a terrible effort for her, finding you last night. Aye, she was like a dead woman for two hours.' She sighed. ''Tis sad, for there ne'er was such a spaewife as Granny in her young days; past and present were as clear as water to her eye. And Beatie, and myself – we dunna ha' the power. Except Beatie a little, when she was wandersome with the fever.'

Abigail said, 'I'm the Stranger, aren't I?'

'Aye,' said Dovey. 'Granny is certain of it. The signs are right.'

'Tell me,' begged Abigail. 'It's very frightening, Dovey. To be me, I mean. Not understanding anything at all.'

Out of the corner of her eye she saw Beatie creep in and sit on the rag rug beside Dovey's bed. Her sallow face was both fascinated and repelled. Dovey looked at her warningly.

'I'll not have any jeering, Beatie,' she said, severely for her. 'We all know verra well, for you've told us a thousand times, that you dunna want the Gift and won't have it; but nevertheless you and your children, should you have any, are in the way of it.'

'Babbies!' cried Beatie disgustedly. 'Who'd want the puling, useless things?'

The Gift was not in the Bow family, but in the Tallisker clan. Mrs Tallisker as a girl had borne the same surname. She had married her cousin, for young men were scarce on Orkney where the sea took so many. It had been the ancestress of both these young people who had been whisked away to Elfland for several years, and then reappeared as mysteriously as she had vanished.

'You see, Abby,' explained Dovey, 'Orkney is a queer old place, where dwarfies and painted men, Picts you might call them, lived long ago, and built great forts and rings of stone where a shepherd might wander and ne'er be seen again. And there are trolls, and spells to be said against them, and the children of the sea who dance on the sands on St John's Eve . . . and it was Granny's seventh grandmother, Osla, who was elf-taken while she was watching the sheep and came back from Elfland with a wean about to be born. And with that wean came the Gift.'

This precious legacy was the gift of seeing the future, of healing, of secret wisdom. The Gift could be handed down by the men of the family, but never possessed by them. With the Gift, Osla's child, fathered in Elfland, had brought the Prophecy.

102

Granny was the greatest spaewife and healer of them all, explained Dovey. But as she grew older the Gift left her, coming only in erratic, puzzling flashes that she could not always understand. She could not, for instance, correctly interpret the Prophecy, although she was sure that Abigail herself was the Stranger.

'It's this way,' explained Beatie gruffly. 'Whenever the Gift looks like breeding right out, a Stranger comes. You can tell the Stranger because he or she always has something belonging to the Talliskers.'

'Well, I haven't,' thought Abigail. 'Granny's barking up the wrong tree this time. It can't be my dress, because Mum said that was an Edwardian curtain I made it from and she's never wrong about fabrics.'

'And the Stranger makes the Gift strong again,' said Beatie. Her turbulent, troubled little face was solemn. 'The blanky thing!'

'Beatie,' reproved Dovey, 'how can you speak that way?'

'Because,' Beatie said crossly, 'even though I dunna want the Gift myself, I know it's true. Oh, aye, I'm dead afeared of it; but I know it's true.'

For an instant Abby thought Beatie was going to confess that several times she had gone unvolitionally into the next century, but instead she muttered, 'You mind when I was sick, Dovey, and I had the dream of Mother's funeral and the yellow fever rag on the door . . .' Here Abigail started, for she, too, had dreamed of a door with a yellow rag tied to the knocker. 'And my three sisters that died of the smallpox came to me, looking as bonny as angels.'

'Well I remember that dream,' said Dovey. 'I feared they had come for you.'

'Those were only dreams,' said Beatie. 'But that night I had a flash, clear as day, and I knew I was no' to die. I didna like to tell you, in case you thought I had the Gift.'

'Whatever did you see, Beatie?' interposed Abigail.

'My own hands,' said Beatie, 'and they were a woman's hands, and there was no ring on them, and they were holding a book, very heavy, with a leather cover. A scholarly book. And I thought then, maybe I winna be an ignorant lass all my life, but get some education like Judah, or even better. I have kept it from you, Dovey; but all must come out now with Granny so low.'

Both Dovey and Beatie seemed to have forgotten Abigail, and she herself was thinking furiously. 'And why shouldn't she? She's brainy, and as determined as a little red devil. This Mr Taylor, who runs the class for promising boys, he must have a feeling for education . . . Perhaps if Beatie went to see him, let him know how much she has learnt, how much she longs to be properly educated . . .'

There was a piercing wail from above.

'I want the chamber-pot, Dovey. Come quick!'

Beatie sprang to her feet. 'I'll go, Dovey, and won't I shove his head in it if he's doing no more than pester us!'

'I'd like to see Granny,' said Abby. 'Please, Dovey.'

The old woman who lay in the small iron four-poster bed was scarcely recognisable. She had a look of ancient and unbearable fatigue, as though all strength had drained out of her. Abigail saw her eyes flickering under the silken brown eyelids.

'Granny,' said Dovey softly, "tis Abby, come to show you she is safe.'

The eyes opened. Light had drained out of them also. The glistening vitality and intelligence, so like that in Judah's eyes, had gone. The dark blue had faded to a bleached slate-grey. Abigail was shocked and distressed.

'Oh, Granny,' she cried, 'do you feel very bad? Oh, Granny, I'm so sorry, but I just had to try to go home.'

The knobbly old hand wavered out. Abigail took it.

The old woman's grip was feeble, and yet firm. She held Abigail's hand lightly but Abigail felt that even if she wanted to take her hand back she would not be able to.

'She hanna the Power, Dovey,' said the dim, rustling voice. 'She isna one of us. But there's something there, something . . . I can feel it strengthening me. Now, Abigail, isna the time for truth come? For you and for us, too, forbye. You dinna come from another country, but from another time?'

Abigail heard Dovey gasp. She told Mrs Tallisker the year of her birth, and Dovey breathed, 'Dear God, is it possible?'

'Hush, Dovey. Tell me true, Abigail, in that far-off time which is yours and not ours, did ye ever hear the name Tallisker, or Bow?'

'No, never,' said Abigail truthfully.

'Your father's name is Kirk? A Scottish name.'

'Yes, but he's half Norwegian. He was born in Narvik, and brought to Aust . . . to New South Wales as a baby.'

'His mother's name?'

'Emma Rasmussen.'

Granny Tallisker asked the same questions about Abigail's mother. But Kathy was fourth generation Australian, and Abigail knew of no blood strain other than English and German amongst her mother's ancestors.

'Yet you are the Stranger,' murmured the old lady. ''Tis very puzzling, Dovey.'

'I'm not, you know,' said Abigail emphatically. 'You've made a mistake. I got here quite accidentally. It was because . . .' she stopped. She had promised Beatie solemnly that she would not ever tell that the younger girl had visited the twentieth century.

'No, no,' said the old woman almost impatiently. 'You are the Stranger; there is nae possibility of mistake.'

Her voice had grown stronger. The hyacinth colour

almost perceptibly flowed back into her eyes. Abigail wondered uneasily if she were withdrawing vitality from her own hand, and she tried to take it away, but could not without a sharp, rude jerk.

Suddenly Dovey spoke rapidly in the broad Orkney dialect. Abigail could scarcely catch a word except 'aye' and 'Beatie' and 'unwed'. Mrs Tallisker was excited.

'Then she's not to die, my clever wee hen! God be praised for that, anyway.'

'I have just told Granny what Beatie saw,' Dovey explained; 'the woman's hands without a ring, and a book in them. And she says that is the first part of the Prophecy proved.'

Abigail was bewildered. She was not interested in the Prophecy. What she wanted to know was how Granny had known where she was held captive. But it didn't seem the time to ask.

'The Prophecy,' explained Mrs Tallisker, 'is for each fifth generation, when it is so ordered that the Gift is at risk. This is the fifth generation from my grandfather's time, when there wunna a Tallisker left but himself, after the Stuart wars in Scotland. Tell Abby the words, Dovey, the while I catch my breath.'

Dovey said in a low reluctant voice, 'It is in our Orkney speech, but it means, "One to be barren and one to die."'

'Well, goodness,' said Abigail, 'I can't see that that's so bad.'

'See, Abigail,' explained Dovey, 'I am the sole child of Granny's son Robert Tallisker who drowned, God rest his soul. And of the bairns of my Aunt Amelia, four died young. Of those who can hand on the Gift to the future, there are now no more than four.'

'You, Judah, Beatie and Gibbie,' said Abigail thoughtfully.

'And of those Beatie is to be barren and will not hand on the Gift,' said Mrs Tallisker.

'But you don't know that!' protested Abigail.

'The ringless hand,' reminded Dovey. 'She saw it herself. She will not wed, and will be childless.'

'I think it's absolutely repulsive,' cried Abigail, 'talking about people as if they were part of some superstitious pattern. It's all right for Beatie not to marry if she doesn't want to, don't you see? But that means one of the rest of you will die.'

'And die young,' said Dovey.

'Don't you care?' cried Abigail. 'Why, it might be you! It might be Judah!' Then realisation struck her. 'Gibbie! You believe Gibbie's going to die, don't you?'

'It might well be the poor little one,' said Dovey gently. 'He hasna made headway since the fever, and it is now seven months since he sickened. His little bones are like sticks, and he hasna put on an ounce, feed him up as we may. But on the other hand, Abigail, it may be myself, as you say. It is your coming that will decide.'

'I've nothing to do with it!' cried Abigail. 'I came here without wanting to and I want to go home. I've a life of my own, and I want to live it. My mother, I miss her, don't you understand?' she said chokily. She thought fiercely, 'I won't cry, I won't.' She waited for a moment, and then said quietly, 'I'm not your mysterious Stranger. I'm just someone who came into your life here in some way that's a riddle to me. But I have to go home, I don't belong here. You must see that.'

'We canna let you go,' said Mrs Tallisker. She had relinquished Abigail's hand and was sitting up against her pillows. Except for her sunken eyes she looked almost like her own dignified strong self again.

Abigail glowered. 'I'll run away again and again till I

find the place where I came into this horrible century; and I'll go, I swear I will.'

'But we canna let you go until you have done whatever it is the Stranger must do to preserve the Gift.' Dovey was distressed. 'Oh, dear Abby, it may only be for a little while and then we will help you go to your own place. We do understand what you feel, that you long for your ain folk, but we canna let you go . . . you are our only hope, you see.'

Abigail said unbelievingly, 'This thing . . . is it so precious to you that you'd do this to me? It . . . isn't Christian.'

'The Gift is not Christian,' said Mrs Tallisker. 'But aye, you have it right, girl. It is so precious to us that we would keep you here for ever if this were ordained to be so.'

'Judah wouldn't let you!' burst out Abigail. 'He's got some gumption, he's a seaman, a grown man . . .' But she could see from their pitying faces that Judah believed in the Gift as strongly as they did.

'Either they're all dotty, or I'm dreaming,' thought Abigail. Her knees wobbled. 'But I'm not dreaming. I'm here, in a little Victorian cottage full of oil lamps and iron pots and funny clothes and paintings of people who lived before Queen Victoria was born. It's real, more real than Magpies, or anything.'

At the thought that she was trapped as efficiently as she had been in that gloomy cavern of the Suez Canal, she sniffed dolorously.

'I can't go my whole life without seeing my mother and father again,' she whispered. 'And truly you are mistaken. I'm not this Stranger of whom you talk. I didn't have anything belonging to the family. I wasn't even wearing anything unusual: just my green dress.'

'Aye,' said Mrs Tallisker, and her voice was so tender, so loving, that chills ran up and down Abby's spine.

'My dress? That had something to do with . . . ?'

All at once she remembered the dream-like conversation she had heard that first terrible, confused, and painful night. Dovey and Granny. Whispers. No mistake. Pattern. Not a needle set to it yet.

She cried, 'Not the dress, the crochet! *The crochet!*'

She saw by glancing from one to the other that she was right.

'The pattern . . . the grass of Parnassus . . .'

'It is a common bog plant in Orkney,' said Dovey.

'The initials,' breathed Abigail. 'A.T. Not Anastasia Tassiopolis but Alice Tallisker . . . I don't know what to say. That crochet – you designed it, you made it . . . but not yet.'

Mrs Tallisker nodded. She had wearied again. The small vitality she had absorbed from Abigail seemed to have leaked away now that Abigail herself was trembling and shocked.

'The crochet brought me here in some way; it was a sort of link between me and Beatie . . . and you've burnt the dress, so now I can never get back, never.'

She felt very much older than fourteen. She felt like an old woman.

It was like the terrible lostness and helplessness she had felt when her father went away. The empty place inside her had swallowed her up. She got up to leave the room. Dovey tried to stop her, but Abigail's stony, hating face made her recoil. She went downstairs, with Dovey limping after her.

Mr Bow looked up with surprise from the marble slab where he was moulding liquorice babies.

'What in the name of fortune are you doing, girl? You're still in your night-rail!'

Abigail looked down without interest at her stiff calico nightdress. It struck her then that this was the kind of

109

clothing she would always wear until she was an old woman and graduated to a flannel gown and a baby's bonnet nightcap like Mrs Tallisker. That was if she survived scarlet fever, cholera, plague, and all the things she had not had shots for.

'Fortunately I have had my polio injections and my smallpox inoculations,' she remarked politely to Mr Bow. The man looked flabbergasted. He wiped his hands on his apron and led her gently away from the door. He put his sticky hand on her forehead, and said anxiously to Dovey, 'Would she be sickening for something, walking about this way in her shift?'

Dovey tried to put her arms around Abigail, but she pushed them away. 'You pretend to be kind, but you're cruel. Your father died and your mother died, and you know how hard it is. But you will keep me away from my home and my friends and my mother and I'll never see her again.'

She felt that somewhere inside her she was sobbing broken-heartedly, but outwardly she was calm.

'I can't trust any of you, except Judah.'

She thought then of Judah as a rock in the wilderness. His strength, his frankness and plainness of speech, his understanding of Beatie's longing for education – why else should he be teaching her Latin, and geometry, too, for all Abigail knew?

'Abby, Granny wants to see you. Please come.'

'I don't want to.'

'It's about your dress.' Dovey faltered. 'I told you an untruth, Abby, and verra ashamed I was. But Granny thought it best. Your dress was not burnt, 'tis hid away, safe as houses.'

Abigail leapt up the stairs two at a time. She burst into Granny's room. Beatie was helping the old woman into a clean wrapper. Abigail's rage was beyond bounds. She opened her mouth to yell at Mrs Tallisker, but the old woman looked at her steadfastly. It was if she were being engulfed by those blue eyes. Her anger melted, and she said, gently and politely, 'Is it true that my dress was not destroyed?'

'True indeed,' replied the old woman tranquilly. 'And when you've done what you were sent here to do I shall give it back to you, and you can return home.'

'But I don't know what I have to do,' said Abigail desperately.

'It will show itself in time,' said Granny.

Abigail begged and pleaded, but Mrs Tallisker was adamant.

'The Gift is more precious than you, or any of us here. It munna be more than a couple of days before we know what you must do.'

'Tell me what it is and I'll do it!' pleaded Abigail.

But Granny shook her head. 'That we dinna know, child. But it will reveal itself.'

'Why don't you know, if you have the Gift?' cried Abigail.

'Because I'm old and the Gift is leaving me –' replied Granny with dignity, 'as is the power of my sight and the strength of my hands. If I could still heal would I not make poor Gibbie as strong as his brother?'

'All very well,' thought Abigail contemptuously, 'but how did you know I was in that warehouse, tied up and helpless?'

'Because you called me, child,' answered the old woman readily, 'and I sent out my mind to search for you.'

Distantly the voice of Gibbie could be heard, cheeping wretchedly.

'I'll see to him,' said Abigail to Beatie. She was half-way up to the attic before she realised that Mrs Tallisker had answered a question she had not asked aloud. She shuddered. Did Judah believe all this stuff? Did Mr Bow?

Gibbie was lying back on his little bed, looking holy. Abigail looked at him critically. No doubt of it, he was a miserable whitebait of a kid, as flimsy within as without, she had no doubt. He opened one eye a slit and peered at her through his eyelashes, and began to wheeze dramatically.

'Don't waste your theatrics on me,' said Abigail.

'Going to the theatre is the devil's work,' said Gibbie in his parson's tone. 'You fall straight into hell fire ten miles down.'

'Sounds fun,' said Abigail. Gibbie blanched.

It was no wonder, thought the girl, that Granny and Dovey thought he would be the one to die. And this conclusion, she knew, would not lie easy on their minds. She recalled Dovey's devotion to the child, her sleepless nights and endless patience with a youngster Abigail felt was as unlovable and obnoxious as a child could get.

The attic had a sloping roof covered with flowered wallpaper. There were framed texts on the walls. In the sharp angle of the ceiling and floor was a small casement window.

'Dunna you open it,' said Gibbie in a fright. ''Twould mean my death of cold, immediate!'

'I'm just looking,' said Abigail. The attic window looked over the back of the house, over midget back yards; 'wee hoosies'; and incredible masses of rubbish: old iron bedsteads, broken hen-coops, rusty corrugated iron. The skillion roof of the Bows' kitchen ran below the window, to extend half over the next yard, where someone had strung a line of deep-grey tattered washing. A small pig

112

was tethered on the roof, rooting listlessly at a heap of rotting cabbage leaves. In the next yard two Chinese with pigtails worked industriously over a steaming copper. *Their* laundry was dazzling white. Baffled by this, Abigail returned to the bed, where Gibbie was watching her with big eyes.

'Why do you look so different from us?'

'You've got me there,' said Abby. 'Haven't you anything to do besides pick your nose? Haven't you anything to read?'

'I dinna read very well, but sometimes Granny tells me stories of the fishermen, and the big storms and such things; and when Judah is home from a voyage he tells me of shipwrecks and rafts, and the forest where the cedar is cut, and how he's going to be master of his own ship, and sail to the Solomons and see the savages.'

'That must be interesting,' said Abigail. The little boy's face had momentarily lost its pinched, old-monkish look, and become vivacious and excited. Then he said in his dreariest tone, 'But I'm going to heaven instead to be with Mamma and the angels, and I daresay that is twice as worthwhile as the Solomon Islands.'

'Poor little rat,' thought Abigail. Then she caught herself: 'I'm going on as if I believe he's going to die, just like the rest of them.' Aloud she said, 'Do you know the story of *Treasure Island?*'

Gibbie's eyes glistened. 'I do not. Can you tell it to me?'

Abby began: 'Once upon a time there was a pirate called Long John Silver . . .'

'But if *he* doesn't die,' she thought, 'there's only Dovey and Judah.' The room seemed to fill with Judah's warmth and liveliness, his boy's joviality and his man's sense of responsibility towards his family. She could almost hear

113

him telling this sick child of tropical forests and coral reefs, never mentioning all the hardships and perils of an apprentice seaman on a coastal brig.

'Won't ye be goin' on?' pleaded Gibbie. 'For I'm fair mad to hear about this pirate.'

'He had a wooden leg,' said Abby absently.

'Oh,' she thought, 'don't let it be Judah; it mustn't be Judah!'

# Chapter 8

In a way, she felt as she had felt when her father went away and left her. Fright, anger and helplessness, the sense of being nobody who could make things happen. But then she had been only ten. Four years of schooling her face to be expressionless, her thoughts to be her private property, had not gone to waste.

After her first despair, she thought, 'I won't let them beat me. If that dress is hidden around the house I'll find it. Or I'll bribe Beatie, or coax Judah, into telling me where it is.'

She had learnt a lot about herself in this new rough world. Her own thoughts and conclusions of just a month before filled her with embarrassed astonishment when she reviewed them.

'What a dummo I was! I knew as much about real life as poor little Natty.'

She stopped being silent and distraught and asked Granny if she could help in the house and the shop until whatever it was that she was fated to do as the Stranger was revealed.

Granny put her arms about her. Orkney folk were an undemonstrative people, as she had realised, and Granny's action touched her. 'My heart aches for you, Abby, but 'twill be worth it, for you as well as the rest of us. It is my duty to see the Gift handed on. I can do no other.'

Abigail nodded gravely. Granny's eyes twinkled. 'And if you are planning on finding your gown, hen, it's nae guid. It's where you'll n'er look for it.'

'Oh, damn you all!' Abigail was furious.

'Fair enough,' said Granny, her eyes still twinkling.

Still, rather than maunder around with nothing to do, Abigail fitted herself into the household routine. She learnt to rake out the shop fire and carry the ash in pails to the ash-pit in the yard. Some of this ash was saved and sifted and used to make soap. Though many of the inhabitants of The Rocks washed themselves, during their rare personal ablutions, with the harsh lye soap, the Talliskers and Bows used it for laundry soap and never applied it to their skins.

'You'd be as chapped as a frost-bitten potato in a week, lass,' explained Granny. They all, even the men, used oatmeal in muslin bags with which to scrub themselves, and as the days went by Abigail noticed her own brown skin taking on the fineness that was characteristic of all the family's complexions.

She scrubbed and dusted, washed and polished the lamp chimneys, and learnt how to set a wick so that the paraffin (which she called kerosene) burnt clear and without odour.

She did approach Beatie about the dress, but the girl said downrightly she had no idea where it was, and would not tell if she did.

'But Beatie, if I could escape to my own time, maybe you could come with me, and go to school, and learn all you want, with no one to discourage you.'

A look of intense yearning passed over the younger girl's face.

'I'd sell my ten toes for it, as ye weel know,' she said,

'but how could I leave Dovey? For she's all in all to me now my mother's gone. Aye, I'd do without anything in life rather than leave Dovey.'

Abigail best liked working in the shop. Very quiet and mild since his last frenzy, Mr Bow was a pleasant companion, though given to bursts of tears, turning away unexpectedly and wiping his eyes on the corner of his apron.

'I'm as right-minded as any man when I don't touch the spirits,' he explained. 'But the pain in my head gets that bad, and hain't it a temptation then to have a halfer and relieve it a little? But I didn't hurt you bad, wench, eh, did I?'

'Only a little, Mr Bow,' Abigail assured him. She said frankly, 'I expect you know that Mrs Tallisker thinks I'm the mysterious Stranger?'

'Don't I just,' he replied, 'and it must be a heart scald for you, kept here amongst folk not your own. But I ain't saying nothing about it, Miss, because I'm skeered to do so, if you must know the truth of it. For 'tis true, you know, the Gift and that.'

'But, Mr Bow,' protested Abigail, 'you're English. You can't believe this Orkney fairy-tale.'

He looked at her sadly. 'I do, dear Miss, and that's a fact. Didn't my pretty 'Melia, when I was a-courting her, tell me that she'd die afore me and leave me with enough sorrow to break my back? I laughed me head off, for you know I was near twenty years older than 'Melia, and in the course of nature it was to be expected that I would be taken afore her. But I said two years of your company, my pretty dear, is worth a lifetime of tears. And I did better than that. Nigh nineteen years we was wed, and never a frown.'

117

Here he turned away quickly.

'Did you ever see Florence Nightingale?' interposed Abigail hurriedly.

He wiped his eyes, turned once more to his patient pulling and slapping of the rapidly congealing toffee over the great hook. 'Nay,' he said 'not to remember like. I mind only filth and the stink of wounds and green water. And then the ship and England. And after a long time I rejoined my regiment and, unfit for active duty as I was, we was posted to New South Wales to the garrison. And there I served out my term, four years agone now. And what I'd do without Granny and Dovey I can't bear to think, for there's Beatrice needs a mother, and Gibbie a-fading away, and myself that mazy sometimes I dunno if I'm on head or heels.'

Abigail realised dolefully that Mr Bow would never cross Granny in order to help her.

But this did not mean that she did not stealthily investigate every available place where her dress might have been hidden. In such a tiny cottage she was rarely alone, and she was abashed and angry when caught scrabbling behind the sacks of sugar in the cellar under the shop.

'It inna worthy of you, pet,' said Granny quietly. Abigail was crimson.

'It's all your fault,' she retorted. 'You took my dress and hid it. I've never before snooped amongst other people's things in my life!'

'And you'll not have to again,' said Mrs Tallisker, mildly, 'for I'll tell ye where the gown is laid away. In Dovey's bride chest, which is locked.'

Abigail groaned. 'You know very well I'd never as much as lift the lid of Dovey's bride chest, let alone break the lock. You're as crafty as a fox; you ought to be ashamed!'

'Aye,' agreed Granny tranquilly, 'but 'tis all in a good cause.'

'I just want to go home, you know,' whispered Abigail.

'You're as restless as a robin, child,' said Mrs Tallisker. 'But 'twill not be long now.'

There was a great difference in Mrs Tallisker. She had, all at once, become older and smaller. Only a few weeks before she had towered, or so it seemed, over Abigail. Now Abigail was almost as tall. Her skin had crumpled more deeply, more extensively, like a slowly withering flower. She could not work as hard as before, but sat more often in the parlour with Gibbie, knitting thick grey socks for Judah.

'Aye,' she said with her sweet smile, as Abigail secretly stared at her, "tis a fearful effort to give out the Power when it has decided to leave. If I could do what I did for you, child, you can give me a little of your time, inna that fair enough?'

'Yes, of course,' said Abigail, but in her heart she was grudging.

Sometimes she sat, pondering, in front of Dovey's bride chest. It was a small, green-painted tin box with an arched lid decorated with faded tulips and rosettes. In there was her key to home, but her sense of honour prevented her from taking a knife and forcing the lid.

'It's ridiculous,' she thought, 'but it's true. I can't touch it. Oh, that Granny! She knows me better than I do myself.'

She had no curiosity about the contents of Dovey's bride chest, knowing that from the age of seven every Orkney girl began to prepare household linen against the day when her hand would be asked in marriage. She thought it would be full of towels and sheets and little muslin bags to hold oatmeal.

The Rocks was an uncomfortable place to be at that

time of the year. As often in Sydney, it was a time of spectacular electrical storms and erratic summer rain. Wild winds snored and spiralled off the Pacific archipelagoes, their fringes sweeping the Australian coast like the edges of cloudy shawls. Judah's ship, *The Brothers*, had been driven onto the mud at Walsh Bay, and needed repairs. Though he was working on her all day, he was permitted to spend the nights at home, and so she saw far more of him than hitherto.

Now that she was familiar with the household routine, Abigail saw that it turned upon Judah's comings and goings as if he were a pivot. He blew into the house like a bracing nor' easterly, and everyone, from the mourning father to Gibbie languishing before the fire in the suffocatingly hot parlour, seemed to absorb vitality from him. He was unlike any boy Abigail had known in her own world. He was just a well-knit, sturdy person of middle height, yet his muscles were of oak, his mind far-reaching and vigorous.

At first Abigail observed him with friendly curiosity. The difference between him and boys of eighteen in her time was that Judah was a man. She thought of the likeable, aimless brothers of many of her friends, without discipline or ambition, and wondered uneasily how it had come to be that they were so different from this son of a poor family, who had done a man's job, and thought it a right rather than a burden, from his fourteenth year.

He was artless and straightforward, with not the slightest interest in the world from which Abigail had so strangely come.

At first she thought he did not believe her when she told him of ships driven by atomic fission – some under the water – and told him that even ferries no longer used steam, but were oil powered.

120

'Oh, aye,' he said, unconcerned. 'I believe you. Hanna I seen the Gift at work so often since I was in arms? My mother knew the very day I would return to dock, fair weather or foul, and would have a plum duff in the pot, for as a lad I was fair crazy for a slice of Spotted Dick. But what you tell me, Abby love, well, 'tis like all the fingle-fangles the Government men prate about – Henry Parkes and all that lot – Federation and free trade, and republicanism. I know 'tis true, but it hanna importance for me. 'Tis here I live, do you see, in 1873, and my labour is here, and my own folk, and I'm thankful to God for both. So that's enough for me.'

'But men landing on the moon!' cried Abigail. 'Don't you think *that's* fantastic?'

'Damned foolishness, I call it,' he said, and flushed. 'Your pardon, Abby, for a word Granny would thicken my ear for, but 'tis no more and no less. What good to man or beast is that bare lump of rock?'

'At least it makes the tides,' snapped Abigail, 'and where would you be without them?'

He laughed. 'True for you, but no man has to go there to press a lever or turn a wheel for that!'

Having failed to interest him in the future, she turned to the past, and asked him was he ever homesick for Orkney, as she knew Dovey was.

'Not I,' he said. 'Why, 'tis the past, and dead and gone. I'm a New South Welshman now, and glad about it, aye, gey glad!' His eyes danced. 'Ah, I'm glad to be alive, and at this minute, I tell ye! There's few enough with my good fortune – for in a month or so I'll be an AB, with a decent wage and prospects. Oh, aye,' he added hastily, in case she felt slighted, 'I'm sure the time you came from is a very grand place to be, but it's no' for me, not for all the tea in China.'

121

The cottage was always noisy when Judah was at home. Either he was doing a sailor's jig with Beatie, twirling Granny in what she called a 'poker', playing tunes on a tin whistle, or giving Gibbie hair-raising pick-a-back rides up and down the twisted stairs. She began to listen for his laugh, his 'Ahoy, who's at home at Bows'?' as he came in, for he had the soft full voice of Dovey and his grandmother, very pleasant to the ear. Other times she would find him, late at night, his bright fair head bent in the circle of light from the paraffin lamp as he corrected Beatie's Latin exercises, or studied his books on navigation.

'For I've a mind to have my own ship one day,' he said cheerfully. 'If Captain Cook could do it, so can I, and sail to the cannibal islands and bring back a cargo of sandalwood.'

'And what will you do when you're rich?' asked Abby laughing.

He gave her his candid blue look. 'I'll take my faither to a fine surgeon and have his trouble fixed, so that he can be happy, and I'll pay a clever tutor to give Beatie all the learning she wants, and I'll buy Dovey a fine silk dress like a princess, and I might give you a white mouse for a pet.'

'Nothing larger or finer?' she asked teasingly.

'Ah, so you'd like a rat? Then I'll catch you one this very night. We have them by the thousand on board *The Brothers*, and the ship's cats are all worn down as small as this with hard work.'

He showed her with finger and thumb.

'Oh, Judah,' she laughed, 'you're a clown. I'll miss you when I go home.'

And all at once it hit her. It was like a physical blow, so that she lost her breath, and could scarcely gasp a 'Good night' before she fled for the stairs.

Dovey was already in bed and asleep. Abigail undressed hurriedly in the dark, flung herself into bed and buried her face in the feather pillow. It was not possible. Love could not pierce one with a dart, envelop one with an unquenchable fire, all those things that old songs said, that the girls at school said. 'I saw him getting off the bus and my knees went. I didn't know what I was doing. I went down the wrong street and left my school-case at the bus stop.' Or, 'I just sort of burnt all over; it was unreal. I couldn't have answered if he'd spoken to me, I was paralytic.'

Mum, talking about meeting Dad. 'We were both swimming. He was thrashing along and ran into me. Boom! Knocked all the wind out of me. He hauled me out of the water like a wet sack. None of your romantic picking me up and carrying me out. And I lay on the sand whooping. Oh, it was squalid, I can tell you. He said "Why weren't you watching where I was going, you knucklehead?" Typical. My fault, mind you. His hair was all plastered down, like yellow seaweed, yuk! I just lay there making noises like an up-chucking cat and looking at his blue, blue eyes, and thinking, "I've met him at last, my own man. Wonder what his name is?"'

My own man! When her mother had said that, so spontaneously and gaily, Abigail had been so embarrassed she marvelled that she had not come out in hives all over. The idea of one's mother coming out with a golden oldie phrase!

But now she saw it was the only phrase there was.

She could scarcely admit it to herself. The most exquisitely delicate sensation touched her, body and mind. The empty place in her heart opened like a flower and was filled.

'I love him,' she thought. 'I love Judah. I've loved him

123

all along, ever since he carried me to the window that first night. And I didn't know.'

She lay awake for hours, in a daze of happiness.

It was like going to another country, seeing landscapes that were not of this world. Yet she had known those landscapes were there: that was why she had always felt empty, incomplete, because she knew they were there and she belonged in them, but she did not know where to look to find them.

The dark room seemed full of diamonds and spangles, as though the light within her was so exuberant it streamed from her eyes and fingers and toes.

The ships moored at the wharves creaked and groaned, hasty footsteps sounded on the cobbles of a nearby lane. In the Chinamen's laundry the mangle thumped. These sounds were drowned by the bim-bam of thunder, and the dark was suddenly wiped over by lightning. She heard Gibbie shriek above, and Dovey instantly stir.

'I'm awake, Dovey,' she said. 'I'll go up to him.'

'Take the cannle, pet,' said Dovey drowsily and thankfully, 'and my red gown.'

Abby stumbled up the stairs. The baggy red-flannel dressing-gown smelt of perspiration and the vinegar Dovey had used to sponge the collar and cuffs. Normally Abby would have been sickened by it. But now she was different. These small things did not seem to matter any more.

'I dunna want you,' snivelled Gibbie, sitting up in bed like a pale owl, his hair a meagre fuzz. 'I want my Dovey.'

'Dovey's so tired,' said Abigail. 'You'll be a good lad and let her have her sleep, won't you?'

'I'm that skeered of lightning,' he sobbed. ''Twill come and get me and grill me like a kipper!'

'It won't if I'm here,' said Abigail confidently. She sat beside him. He smelled sickly and looked like a little death's-head in the candlelight. And Abigail found herself thinking, 'It's a good thing, though. Now Dovey and Judah are safe.'

For an instant she remembered her mother's dark dewdrop eyes, as she said, 'You don't know how powerful love can be', and she thought how strange it was that love had made her both callous and tender. She did not care if this child died. Though she had never liked him, she had not wanted to deprive him of his life. But now, if his death meant that Judah lived, then she did not care a jot if he died.

At the same time she did what would have made her skin creep a day or so before: she put her arms around his shivering, bony little body and held him comfortingly.

She thought, 'I think I could even do the same for foul Vincent, the way I feel now.'

'Want to do Number One,' said Gibbie. She brought him the chamber-pot; put it away on the wash-stand again.

'Lie down now and go to sleep. I'll keep the lightning from hurting you,' she said.

'Are you a witch?' asked Gibbie, big-eyed. 'Beatie said you wunna.'

Abigail considered. 'No, I'm not. But I'm very good with thunder and lightning. Shall I tell you some more about Long John Silver and the other pirates?'

But the little boy was asleep in a few moments. The storm had boiled out to sea; she saw its last rip of light across the dark clouds on the horizon. The rain-glass was falling, Judah had said that evening. Would rain keep his ship from sailing? She wished that a hurricane would blow and keep him at home for a week. She stood for a while outside the room where Judah and his father slept. She did not wish to be with him; it was enough to know that he was there.

The rain was very heavy. It crashed down the slopes of

Flagstaff Hill and some feared that the new Observatory itself would come sliding down and perch itself like Noah's Ark on the edge of the cliff. It poured off the High Rocks in torrents and drenched the rat-ridden houses that overhung the alleys. The alleys themselves ran like storm channels. Then the sun would blaze out for a day or two; the air would be full of steams and stinks; people would get out with brooms made of twigs or thick splinters bound in a bush, and sweep away the muck.

Another time Abigail would have been outraged that a city already large and prosperous could tolerate such wretchedness on its front step. But now all the rain meant was that Judah was often at home. She spoke to him little. She helped Dovey wash his wet clothes that reeked of tar and seaweed, turning them constantly as they dried before the kitchen fire.

"'Twas at a time like this that Aunt 'Melia and the others took the fever,' said Dovey. 'For the water gets tainted, and even the gentility die.'

But death seemed a long way from Abigail. Her days seemed filled with richness. She did not ask questions of herself, why she felt this enchanted calm, why she no longer fretted about her mother, her home in that other place. She scarcely thought. She just felt, and lived from day to day.

The coming of love was one thing. Yes, it had hit her like a thunderbolt, as other girls and her own mother had described. But what she felt of love itself seemed different from what she had heard and read. She did not long to touch him or be touched by him. Perhaps, she thought, that comes later.

Now, her whole body and mind and emotions had become exquisitely sensitive and delicate. The simple fact of his physical reality was enough to make her world different. To listen to him, to look at him, occasionally to brush past in the narrow passageways of the cottage, this was enough. More would be unbearable. She looked with intense and uncomplicated joy at the golden glint along his jawbone, his close-set ears, the capable width between thumb and forefinger. These seemed marvellous to her.

She was content with loving. She had not thought about being loved in return, though she believed that surely it must be a law of nature that sooner or later he would look up and see her as she saw him, the only one, the precious one.

There seemed no reason to talk to the others, so she did not speak, unless it was necessary. Perhaps they would believe she was just sulking about being kept a virtual prisoner.

Dovey's shattered thigh pained severely in the wet weather. Granny had taken her into her own room, to rub the girl's leg when the pain was worst.

'For I still have a little of the healing touch,' she explained.

Beatie had gone back to her own bed. She was supposed to help Abigail attend to Gibbie, if he needed someone in the night; but the little girl slept like one dead. So the days went past, and on many nights Abby climbed the attic stairs to the sick child and tried to be kind and tolerant with him. She could not help feeling that his insatiable desire for sympathy and attention was not related to his illness, but to his loss of his mother and his constant brooding on death. And how was she to explain these things to people who had never heard of psychology?

She and Beatie had been down to the market to buy vegetables and meat. It was a fine day; the people were out in crowds. She had enjoyed the outing, seeing the old-clo' shops with the wheeled racks of tattered garments outside, the cobbler with a tall Wellington boot hung as a sign above his door, the itinerant cooks with their charcoal braziers – cooking and selling sausages, scallops, baked potatoes, haddocks, chitterlings – positioned every few yards along Argyle and Windmill streets.

Then, almost out of a blue sky, down had come another summer downpour. The girls had run like hares, but they were soaked, both having dragged off their shawls to cover the goods in case of damage.

They were in their bedroom, changing their clothes, when Beatie all at once said, 'I have to talk to you, Abigail.'

'Talk away,' said Abigail cheerfully. She had been aware that Beatie had been more difficult during the last few days, flying into tantrums, bitter about school, churlish even with Dovey.

Judah had threatened to flatten her ears for her, though he had said it with his usual sunny smile.

'What you need, my lass, is an outing. I'll tell ye, I hae the very thing, and we'll take Dovey and Gibbie too, if the lad's fit enough. We'll go cockling next Sabbath . . . I'll get a lend of a dory, and we'll go maybe right across to Billy Blue's Point!'

But Granny was downright about Gibbie's unfitness to go into the open air, and the sea wind at that, and Dovey murmured that she'd never get down Jacob's Ladder at Walsh Bay with her leg as stiff as it was.

'But 'tis a grand idea, Judah, and Abby will enjoy it, isn't that true, hen? And Beatie will be clean out of her mind, she loves an outing so.'

But now, in the bedroom, Beatie said gruffly, 'You! You're stuck on him, inna that right?'

Abigail had been humming happily. Now she felt as though her blood flowed backwards, so fearful was the sense of privacy breached, of dignity defiled. She stammered, 'I don't know what you mean.'

'Dinna try to hide it from me,' said Beatie. 'I seen it in your face. Look at you now, red as a radish. You're stuck on him, my brother Judah.'

'You mind your own business!' cried Abigail.

'Blind me if it inna my business!' retorted Beatie.

Abigail pulled her shift over her head. In its depths she managed to compose her face, force her outrage to subside.

She pulled down the shift and fastened the tapes of her drawers.

'And suppose you're right, what's the matter with that? Not that I'm saying you're right!'

'Because Judah thinks you're just a child, like me. That's one thing. And the other thing is he's promised.'

'Promised,' whispered Abigail. 'What is promised?'

'Are you daft? He's betrothed to Dovey. He's always been promised to her.'

It was as if the light had diminished. Abigail finished dressing, brushed her damp hair and tied it back. She did all these things automatically, her eyes fixed on Beatie's face.

'Stop girning at me!' ordered Beatie testily. 'What else did you expect? Dinna Judah lame her, when she was but a wean, flitter-brained scamp that he was? Not every man wants a lame wife, so he owes her something. But no matter about that. How could he help loving Dovey, beautiful and good as she is?'

'In my time she wouldn't be thought beautiful,' said Abigail, and was immediately ashamed.

'And in this one you're no oil painting,' snapped back Beatie, 'and neither am I, come to that. But I'm telling you now – Judah belongs to Dovey, and they'll marry as soon as he's out of his time.'

129

'But I've never seen him kiss her or anything,' said Abigail half to herself. 'How could anyone guess they are promised?'

'Kissing! That's no' for Orkney folk,' cried Beatie haughtily. 'We keep our feelings to ourselves.'

'Not you, I notice!' flashed Abigail.

'And anyway,' continued Beatie, 'such things are for after the betrothal, when Judah is out of his time, and is old enough to wed, and gives her a ring. She's to have a garnet in a band of gold – real gold.'

'Groovy,' said Abigail numbly.

'I dinna ken what that means,' said Beatie gruffly, 'but I can tell by your mug it's no compliment. I'm telling you straight, I'll not have you come between them. I'll break your head first.'

'Be quiet!' said Abigail, in so cold a voice that Beatie faltered. Her fiery gaze dropped, and she muttered, 'I hanna any right to speak like that. I ken no other way but to bluster, you see, Abby, because it's the way of folks about here.'

Abigail was silent.

'Nobody's going to make Dovey unhappy,' said Beatie sullenly. 'Nobody. Not while I'm around. Granny'd let her lose Judah if it meant saving the Gift. The Gift comes first with Granny, but it dinna with me! And Dovey's sae gentle – she'd never stand up for her rights, even if her heart broke.'

'Has Dovey noticed too, then?' asked Abigail. Beatie shook her head. 'She hanna mentioned anything. Well, then,' she said, with a return to her previous aggressive manner, 'what will you do about it?'

'This,' said Abigail. She seized Beatie by the shoulders and shook her with such violence that when she let her go, the little girl fell on the floor.

130

She gaped at Abigail, not knowing whether to screech maledictions, or leap at the older girl like an infuriated monkey.

'You're a stirrer, that's what you are,' said Abigail. 'Don't you breathe a word of this to Dovey or I'll break *your* head. You don't know that what you said has a word of truth in it.'

'Granny will know,' said Beatie, half tearful, half triumphant.

'Yes, and I'm going to see her, right now,' said Abigail.

# Chapter 9

The old lady removed her brass-rimmed spectacles and put aside her knitting.

'Ah, there you are, pet,' she said. 'I've been expecting you this last day or two.'

Abigail sat down beside Mrs Tallisker's chair and leant her head on her knee. The touch of the work-hardened hand on her hair was dear and familiar to her.

'You feel that something verra frail and precious, maybe like a china cup, has been chipped and cracked, is that so, Abby?'

Abigail thought about that.

'No,' she said at last, 'it hasn't been spoiled or changed. I just didn't want her – Beatie – or anyone, to look at it because it was private.'

The hand went on stroking.

'I suppose I'm too young to know anything about – about falling in love,' said Abigail humbly. She knew she could never have spoken like this to her mother. She would have died in torment rather than say such a thing to any of the girls at school. It seemed to her now that they were just a bold-mouthed, sniggering rabble of children, too old to be innocent, too young to be fastidious.

'But I suppose that's not fair, either,' she thought. 'How do I know what they feel in their hearts? They talk like that because other kids think they're freaks if they don't.'

'It wouldna be for me to say that you're too young to know true love, Abby,' said Granny tranquilly, 'for I was wed at fifteen myself.'

'And you've not forgotten what it's like?' asked Abigail, amazed.

'Look into my eyes,' said Granny. She took Abigail's chin in her hand and made the girl look steadfastly at her. The cloudy blue of the old woman's eyes cleared, widened, became a sky with clouds running over it like lizards over a wall, a sea far below, leaping, boiling, a marvellous blue-green.

'Like a mallard drake's neckband.' She heard Granny's voice far, far away, hardly distinguishable from the squealing of the birds, white and dark birds whirling in to and out from precipices that stood like walls and battlements.

'Guillemots, sea-shag and terns,' said Granny. 'Look at yourself, lass.'

Abigail was no longer herself. She was someone else. A dark-brown braid streaked with blond fell over her left shoulder almost to her waist. Her hands were red and chapped. She wore a coarse ankle-length black skirt and a white apron. The very eyes through which she looked were different – clearer, further-seeing, and, she instinctively knew, desperate and wild.

'My own e'en,' said Granny, 'when I was eighteen, new-widowed.'

Down that giddy steep Abigail gazed, her whole body thirsting to thrust itself out on that wild wind that whirled the birds down to the sea and up again in tatters and ribbons and shoals of small living bodies; to fall like a stone amongst the black shining reefs and the ever-tossing serpentine arms of the kelp.

'I can't, I can't!' cried Abigail, and her voice was different, her words in a dialect she did not know yet understood. 'There are the bairnies, there are my old

133

parents and yours, Bartle. I cannot come and leave them without a care, I must live on, in spite of pain.'

'I can't bear it,' whispered Abigail. 'I can't bear it!'

In a second she was back in the parlour. Mrs Tallisker, her eyes very bright, was gripping her hands.

'Are you all right, Granny?' panted Abigail. The intensity of her feeling had not left her; she felt she had been through a lifetime of happiness and woe.

'Yes,' said the old woman. She seemed revivified, her bent back straightened, her faded eyes glistening with triumph and excitement.

'Aye, that was a good flash, like a sky full of lightning! Like the old days when past and future were spread out before me like a field of flowers.'

'Was I you?' breathed Abigail. 'Yes, I was you! And Bartle was your husband.'

'Drowned off the Noup like his son Robert. Near nineteen, he was, like his grandson Judah Bow. Aye, the young can experience true love, and true sorrow, and true selflessness too.'

'I don't think I could,' faltered Abigail, 'be unselfish, I mean.'

Mrs Tallisker looked at her with something like scorn.

'If you love truly, you will also know how to live without the beloved, no matter whether you lose him to death or some other.'

Abigail felt helpless and anxious. 'But I don't think I'm good enough to be like that. Maybe when I'm older . . .'

'Age has naught to do with it, Abby,' returned Mrs Tallisker.

'But,' faltered Abby, 'already I feel jealous of Dovey.' She was ashamed. 'When I was shaking Beatie . . .'

The old woman laughed heartily. 'You shook Beatie? 'Twill do that one a world of good.'

134

'Yes,' confessed Abigail, 'I shook her till her tonsils rattled. But all the time I was wishing it was Dovey. It was horrible, like a kind of black oil smeared over everything. I'm afraid, Granny – that I'll be nasty to Dovey, say something cruel. And I don't want to.'

'And why, Abby? Because you like poor Dovey so much, and she hasna done you anything but kindness?'

'Yes, that,' said Abigail, 'but mostly because I don't want to make Judah unhappy, ever, and he would be if anyone hurt Dovey.'

Mrs Tallisker leant over and kissed Abigail's cheek lightly.

'You'll do, my honey.'

She would say no more, but asked Abigail to fetch the lamp and light it.

'And send Beatie to me, hen.'

Beatie went in glowering and came out snivelling. She joined Abigail at the kitchen table where the girl was scrubbing potatoes in a dish of water.

'Granny said I was to be civil to you, and I will; but 'tis not for your sake! So if I smile at you, 'tis from the teeth outwards!'

Abigail sighed. 'I hope it rains on Sunday, so we can't go cockling. Because it will be hell with you glaring at me with steam coming out of your ears.'

'It inna fair!' said Beatie, crimson with wrath and tears. 'Granny said if I didna behave sweet and kind to you she'd give me a look. And if it inna any better than the one I got ten minutes agone, I dunna want to live to see it. And she said I wasna to give as much as a hint to Dovey that you're mooning over my brother Judah.'

'If you'd hurt Dovey that way, then you don't love Dovey as you say you do,' said Abigail sharply. 'You just watch your tongue, because I for one am sick of it.'

135

Beatie turned to her forlornly. 'Well, I ken it is sharpened both ends, but your ain inna much better, Abby, all said and done.'

'What did Granny say to you,' asked Abby, 'to upset you so?'

'She said,' confessed Beatie forlornly, 'that on Sunday Judah would know for true whom he loves, and oh, Abigail, I'm afeared it might be you.'

For one moment Abigail's heart filled with bliss. It blazed up and it was gone, she did not know why. All she felt then was a premonitory sadness, not a child's disappointed sadness, but something sterner and more adult. But this was not a thing about which she could speak to Beatie. It was as private as love. She knew now why her mother had been silent all those years about her hurt and loneliness.

'Well, then,' she said composedly to Beatie, 'at least we know that Sunday will be a fine day and we'll go cockling.'

'Will you promise me, solemn, that you won't let Dovey get hurt?' pleaded Beatie.

Abigail thought about that. 'I can't promise it any more than Granny can promise it. But I don't *want* Dovey to get hurt in any way, and that's for true.'

Beatie considered this. 'Verra well,' she said grudgingly. 'But I'll keep my eye on you. Sharp!'

Dovey prepared them a picnic basket. Her excitement over the beauty of the day, the pleasures in store for them, the feast of cockles they would have that night and on the morrow, seemed almost as if, lame as she was, she frolicked with honest joy at the thought of someone else's good fortune. Inside her Abigail felt a bitter humiliation. If Judah thought of her as a child, as Beatie had once said, Dovey thought of her as even more of one. Even if Dovey had guessed her love for Judah, she had no jealousy towards her. But perhaps she didn't know. Gentle and good as she was, she was not as sharp-witted as Beatie or Gibbie.

Abigail gave Dovey's bride chest a spiteful kick. But that made her feel she *was* a child after all. Heavy at heart, she went down the crooked stairs and through the shop. Mr Bow had banked the great open fire, as he always did at night. A downy blanket of grey ash lay over the winking, slow-breathing fire that drowsed in the depths of the immense log at the back of the chimney. Once a month a log was hauled with chains through a little trapdoor specially built in the side of the house next to the fireplace.

Mr Bow sat on the bench beside this sleeping fire, his hands dangling between his legs. Abigail bade him good-bye but he did not answer.

'I'm not gey happy about him,' confessed Judah as they went through The Cut and over The Green. 'His spells are more frequent, there's no denying. But there's no drink in the house, and he's amenable to Granny. Come now, Beatie, you've a lip like a jug. Cheer up, lass, all will be well!'

But Beatie was fidgety and capricious, running ahead of them through the empty Sunday streets, short with Abigail, impudent to Judah, sometimes sullen, sometimes curvetting and prancing like an urchin, vanishing down side lanes and bobbing out at them again, until Judah caught her by the tails of her pinafore and said, 'Will ye take hold of yourself, hen? I'm weary already of ye jumping about like a nag with a chestnut under its tail. Now, quieten down, for once we get in the boat you'll have to turn into a mouse, and you might as well start practising now.'

Beatie meekly took his hand. They walked ahead of Abigail towards what she knew as Darling Harbour, but

137

which The Rocks people still called Cockle Cove.

Occasionally Beatie turned round and glared at Abigail, as though warningly. And, when Judah was not looking, Abigail glared back, knowing what Beatie meant to convey to her.

'Monkey-face,' thought Abigail. 'Blanky little watchdog!'

Several ladder-like wooden stairways ran down to the beaches and slipways below Miller's Point. The beaches were littered with the refuse of ships – broken gear, rotted rope, rusty iron things half-sunken in the sand and gravel. There was a fearful smell of rotted fish and vegetables from a mountain of muck where the Pittwater boats that brought the northern farmers' produce to the markets dumped their unsold cargoes. Children and old women rooted amongst this garbage for anything edible.

The little boat rocked in a foot or so of water. The girls took off their shoes and stockings and waded out. Judah was already barefooted.

'Get in and be smart about it!' he ordered.

Abigail and Beatie climbed in, and Judah pushed the dory off the sand-flat, running alongside till she was well afloat, and then jumping in and taking the oars. With a couple of strong pulls he had them out in deeper water. Cockle Bay stretched to the south, and beyond their bow were the headlands of the North Shore, bronze green and forested, with faint chalk smudges of domestic smoke drifting up from what looked to Abigail like isolated settlements. Only North Sydney seemed fully built upon, though it was eerie to see it without the Bridge's mighty forefoot coming down upon Milson's Point.

What took Abigail's eye was not the majestic half-wilderness of the North Shore, which she had known as a twin city as tall-towered as Sydney, but the Harbour itself.

'The ships, the ships!' she shouted. 'Hundreds . . . thousands of ships!'

For the Harbour was an inhabited place. Barges with rust-brown sails, busy little river ferries with smoke whuffing from tall stacks, fishing-boats and pleasure boats with finned paddle-wheels, sixty-milers, colliers, towering-masted barquentines with sails tied in neat parcels along what Abigail thought of as their branches – every type of vessel imaginable: huddled in coves, lying askew on slip-ways and beaches, skipping before them over the water, rocking gaily, or slowly and grandly, at buoy or wharf berth.

'What did ye expect, then?' snapped Beatie. 'Cows?'

Abigail, entranced at the magnificent sight, scarcely heard her; but Judah frowned at his sister.

'Whoa, now, lass, what's wi' ye? Is that any way to talk to a guest, and our own Abby at that? Mind your manners, I'm telling you!'

Beatie turned her face away, lip poked out, eyes full of angry tears, which Judah ignored. Abigail rose to her knees, crying, 'It's marvellous! I never dreamt it could be like this!'

'Sit down!' ordered Judah, 'or you'll have us all in the salt. Look overboard and see yon fellow.'

Abigail gingerly sat down, and looked where he pointed. She saw a large shark, with an eye like a willow leaf, cruising three metres below them. A cloud of sprats fled before it. But the green eye was fixed on the boat.

Beatie looked at the shark with a shudder and yet a certain satisfaction.

'No doubt,' reflected Abigail, 'she's imagining me falling overboard.'

'There's *The Brothers*,' said Judah, jerking his head towards a sturdy two-masted brig, very shabby. 'She's square-rigged on both masts. Handy for the coastal trade.'

Abigail asked what these hosts of coastal vessels carried.

'Coal from Newcastle,' said Beatie instantly, 'cedar from the northern rivers, whale oil from the whale station at Eden, and wool from up and down the coasts for the clipper ships to take to England.'

She looked triumphantly at Abigail. 'And what do they carry in your time, then?'

'I don't think there *are* many ships,' said Abigail. 'Things like wool come in trains.'

'We've got steam trains,' said Beatie proudly.

'These would be electric or oil-driven, I think,' said Abigail, 'and then a lot of goods come overland in huge semi-trailers . . . that's a kind of horseless carriage,' she added hastily.

Judah listened politely. 'Seems a sad waste of good money when the sea and the wind are free for all,' he remarked.

Judah's complete lack of interest in the marvels of the future cheered Beatie instantly, and Abigail, no longer irked by the sullen ill-temper of her young companion, gave herself up to the joy of the day.

They drifted past innumerable coves, some a rich green with mangrove swamps, empty of all but a tall white heron picking around in the mud, others already claimed by a little ship-yard, a spindly jetty, a half-ribbed whale-boat skeleton on the slips.

Though Abigail had learnt to know the Harbour and its endless bays from her crow's nest at the top of Mitchell, she had long since lost her sense of direction as the dory nosed around the rock inlets, the warm airs sometimes bringing a Wanderer butterfly, or once a Black Prince cicada, a tinselly creature that clung to the bow with hooked feet, creaked once or twice, and flicked away towards land.

Under cliffs dribbling water, Judah pulled in towards a crescent of beach, dragged up the boat a little way, and jabbed the anchor into the mud.

'I'm hungry, I'm hungry!' cried Beatie, hopping out.

'No, cockles first, while the tide's low,' commanded Judah. He took three wooden pails from the dory. 'Tuck your skirts up. The Dear knows I dunna want you both dripping all over me on the trip home.'

He showed Abigail how to find the breathing hole, and sometimes the track of the cockle, and dig for the shellfish with a stick. Beatie stayed close to her brother, and for much of the time Abigail wandered around alone on the cool, faintly sucking sand. A kind of certainty had fallen over her that this day was to be her last in 1873. She could no longer doubt the Gift, and Granny had told Beatie that this day Judah would know whom he loved. She did not know how this would come about, but she knew that it would.

'And it won't be me,' she thought. Her pail full now, she put it in the shade of a tree, and wandered by herself amongst the rocks, shoaly falls from the cliffs, their crevices filled with driftwood, empty crab-shells, dead and dry starfish and sea-eggs.

In the heat there was uncanny silence, as though the sea itself was too exhausted to sigh or murmur. And in this silence she heard the sounds of farewell.

She sat amongst the fallen cities of the rocks and watched Judah and Beatie, high on the beach, lighting a campfire. Beatie filled a billycan at the spring seepage on the cliff, and once or twice Judah went out and towed the now-afloat dory nearer the shore. The tide was rising fast, with a long whispering *hahhhhh*.

141

The billy must have boiled, for Beatie came running to get her. The little girl's face, though she wore a cabbage-tree hat, as did Abigail and Judah, was scorched with sunburn.

'You've been doing it again!' she accused.

'Doing what?'

'Staring at him. I seen you, sitting on the rocks like a mermaid, staring and gawking.'

Abigail said nothing, but scowled at her and stalked ahead along the beach. A big old redgum, almost one with the sandstone rocks, sheltered them as they ate, hats pulled over their eyes to keep out the sea-dazzle. Judah talked idly of his work: 'Ten bob a month and found, but 'twill be grand pay when I'm an AB.'

Abigail translated this into dollars, couldn't believe the answer, and then remembered that loaves were a penny each, and that Granny often bought a whole fresh fish for twopence. She remarked that being 'a boy' on a coaster seemed to equate with being a man for a boy's pay and status. Judah laughed.

'Well, a boy's a boy, no doubt of that, and he's kept in his place. Me, now, when I started nigh four years ago I brought the food along from the galley and, by jings, I waited till the men had taken their share before I ventured to help myself. Swept the fo'c'sle, took the dishes back to the galley, learnt to know my place right smart after a thick ear or two from one of the crew.'

It seemed to Abigail it would be a hard life, even for a hefty fourteen-year-old as Judah must have been. A boy worked cargo like the rest of the crew, always went aloft to furl the highest sail, and never ventured to offer an opinion during fo'c'sle talk. On the other hand, he was expected to smoke a pipe or chew tobacco.

'Yuk!' said Abigail.

'And sink your quota of rum when you're ashore with the men,' added Judah. 'But Granny – wouldna she skin me alive if she caught me at it and, any old road, I've no taste for either. And I promised Mother besides, so that clinches it.'

He yawned. 'Come on, lassies, let's awa'. I'll show you a pretty place or two, Abby, if you fancy.'

But Beatie wanted to climb the rocks and scramble out onto a little peninsula of grass and pink pigface to be king of the castle, as she said.

'You'll do as I say. Time to move,' he said, stamping out the fire, and gathering up their belongings to put in the basket.

'I want to stay here and paddle,' said Beatie. 'And I'm sick of the boat, up and down, up and down, and nothing to see but water and places with no people in them. I want to play Robinson Crusoe!'

'I don't mind staying a while longer –' began Abigail, but Beatie turned on her roughly. 'Your opinion inna asked! On this voyage you're only the boy!'

Abigail laughed, but Judah took hold of Beatie, gave her a little shake and said sternly, 'What's up with ye today, ye wee smatchit? You've been girning and groaning pretty near since we left home. Are you ailing?'

'I just want to play Robinson Crusoe,' muttered Beatie. Suddenly she aimed a kick at Judah's bare shin.

'Right, that does it,' said her brother. 'You've a temper like a ferret today and I'll stand nae more of it. Stay here and play Robinson Crusoe, while I take Abby for a little row. Get in the dory, Abby.'

He put a wet sack over the cockles and cautioned Beatie: 'Now, see the sun dunna get on them, or they'll all die afore we get them home to Granny. Or do you wish to change your mind and come with us?'

143

Beatie glowered at him, and he said, 'Stay here then, ye self-willed brat. Dovey's too soft wi' you and Gibbie both. We're off – how do you like that?'

'I dunna care a blanky damn!' screamed Beatie, wading out a little way into the water and shaking her fist at them. 'I hope the boat sinks.'

'No, you don't,' yelled back Judah, laughing. 'You play Robinson Crusoe there for a while, while I show Abby the Harbour. We'll be back before Man Friday comes to eat you up!'

Beatie sat down at the water's edge, her arms around her knees, scowling.

'If she could hurl thunder and lightning she would,' Judah laughed. 'Rest easy, Abby. She'll be as sweet as pie when we come back to get her.'

The dory skidded softly over the water that was coloured like a glass marble, here a clear streak and a sun-speckled sand-bar plain to be seen, there dark blue like polished stone.

'Perhaps we shouldn't have left her . . .' began Abigail, but Judah shushed her. He pulled out into the stream and around the edge of the little peninsula that Beatie had wanted to climb. Waterbirds of all kinds flew up from the brown pocked terraces sluiced with translucent water. A glistening native bee landed on Judah's hand, and Abigail leant forward to brush it off.

'No, no, she'll go in the water. She hasna sting, so don't fret.'

He went on rowing, and in a moment the bee arrowed back to the shore.

'I ha'e a great liking for this land,' he said. 'Man hasna spoiled it yet, not even with steam factories and all the dirt the rich make around them.'

He shipped the oars and sat looking about. Abigail peeped from under the brim of her hat at his brown face

144

shining with sweat, his strong calves and calloused feet. As she peeped, thinking herself unobserved in the shadow of the hat, he reached out and playfully caught her foot with his prehensile toes.

She jumped and blushed.

'What's the matter, Abby? For you seem sad today.'

'I think – I think –' She swallowed. Surely she wasn't going to cry? She looked away. 'I think this is my last day.'

'Did Granny say so?'

'No.'

'Well, then?'

Abigail managed a smile. 'I have gifts of my own, you know.'

'Ah, Abby love, don't go! Not to that grievous world you've described. Stay here with us.'

His arms were around her. Her hat fell off into the water and floated away. His cheek rubbed against hers, and she put up her hand and stroked his face.

'Why, Abby, dinna weep, you must not, what's there to weep about on this bright day?'

But she couldn't stop. A huge shameful gulping hiccup came out of her. Judah grinned.

'Don't laugh at me, damn you!' cried Abigail.

'Why, Abby –' he said, as though astonished. 'My little one, my Abby.'

Now, although Abigail had no regular boy friend, she had had her share of kisses, everything from the sudden whack on the lips with what appeared to be a hot muffin, to the lingering pressure of a hairy sardine. She had been half-devoured by someone who had been watching too many Italian films, but when her nose got into the act as well, she had stamped on the kisser's foot and alienated him for ever. She had had ear-biters and eyebrow-lickers, and she cared for none of them.

But this was quite different. Her body went off on its

145

own, yielded and clung and moulded itself to Judah's, her head whirled, and so exquisite a melting sensation arose in her middle she thought she was going to die. She could have stayed there under his kiss for ever, but it was he who drew away, breathing quickly. His face was red, his eyes downcast; he seemed not to want to look at her.

'Oh, Abby,' he said hoarsely, 'it were wrong for me to kiss you in such a way.' He stopped and said with difficulty, 'For a little while I felt – I didna know what I felt. Here you're but a bairn, yet I thought for a moment you were a woman grown. And you *were* a woman grown.'

He gazed at her helplessly. 'It were wrong of me, and yet I canna feel regret.'

She whispered, 'I love you, Judah.'

He gazed at her, silent and perturbed, and she saw in his candid eyes that he had no answer.

She remembered then what Mrs Tallisker had said that if one loved truly, one could exist without the loved one. Her whole body cried out for the few frail blisses she had known – to be able to look at him, listen to him, be kissed as if she were a woman and not a child.

And she thought in anguish, 'If I were older I'd know what to say. But I don't.'

She could only say what was in her heart. 'Don't worry, Judah; I know about Dovey. What I feel about you, well . . . that's my worry, not yours.'

He took her hand and held it between his two large ones. 'But it is my worry, Abby, because now I'm in a swither, I dunno what I feel . . .'

From the little peninsula off which the dory was drifting and circling came a sound like an enraged sea-hawk. Abigail jumped, frightened and dislocated.

''Tis Beatie. She's seen.'

Beatie was up on the tumbled rocks. Her small figure

146

seemed to be doing a war-dance. She picked up a stone and threw it with all her might. It fell far short of the boat, but Judah looked disturbed. He took up the oars.

'She wouldna tell poor Dovey, surely,' he muttered. 'The Dear knows I don't want to distress poor little Dovey.'

They were silent until they pulled in to the beach. The tide was now half full, clear green water sliding in to the foot of the redgum, where Beatie stood waiting with the three pails of cockles. Judah threw out the anchor and jumped ashore.

'You!' said Beatie in a voice shrill with rage. 'I saw!'

'Keep it to yourself then,' he said shortly. 'For I dunna want Dovey upset. Take one of the pails to the boat, there's a good lass.'

'Take it yourself!' spat Beatie.

'Right, I will,' he said. He took all three pails, heaved them into the boat, and said to Abigail, 'Move up while I get this wildcat aboard.'

He held out his hand to help Beatie. She flew at him, punched him in the chest, hammered on the arm with which he held her off. Half angry, half laughing, he said, 'Will ye stop it, ye wee devil? Stop it!'

'I'll punch ye yeller and green!' screeched Beatie. 'To do such a thing to Dovey, who trusts you like she trusts God himself!'

He picked her up by the back of the dress, held her kicking and flailing like a maddened cat, and said, 'You've got it wrong, Beatie. There's naught between Abby and me, and Abby will tell you so.'

He put her into the boat. The child subsided into wild sobs.

Abby ventured to put a hand on her shoulder, but Beatie flung it off.

147

'You're a bad girl! We should have left you in the Suez Canal; it would have suited you grand.'

Judah shipped the oars, leant forward and shook Beatie violently.

'Dunna you speak that way of Abby, when you know nothing of what passed between us. For you're wrong. I'm telling you true, hen!'

Beatie was pale. 'That you could be such a Judas, my own brother! Dovey, expecting to be wed by January, with her bride chest full and her ring chosen, and the down payment made! Don't speak to me, either of you. I'm fair sick to the belly with disgust.'

# Chapter 10

It was a long, wretched trip home against the tide. Beatie sat huddled, her hands over her ears, and would not listen to a word.

''Tis not new,' said Judah ruefully. 'She's as cross-grained a bairn as ever drew breath. And she's been worse since the fever, and Mother's death. Fanciful, and as obstinate as a mule when she gets a maggot in the head about anything.'

'And Dovey,' he sighed, 'she's trusting and innocent as a bairn. I wouldna like that tender heart to be bruised by me, when already I have gi'en her so much suffering, hare-brained young rip as I was.'

Beatie, who had been listening through her fingers, growled, 'Dovey wunna want you now; you're not true to her!'

'All this fuss over a kiss!' said Abigail, vexed.

'A kiss may not mean over much in your time, for the Dear alone knows what you think good or honourable,' cried Beatie. 'But 'tis different for us. And dunna tell me it was a brother's kiss, for I were watching!'

She covered her ears again.

'She won't say anything,' said Abigail. 'She adores Dovey. She wouldn't say anything to hurt her. You'll see.'

'In this mood,' said Judah, 'she'd do anything. She'd jump out the window if she'd a mind to spite someone by it.'

So they returned to the landing-place below Miller's Point. As soon as the bow touched sand, Beatie jumped out, still looking sullen and resolute.

'I have to tell my mate the dory's safe back,' said Judah, 'and he and I will bring up the cockles to the house directly. Hearken now, Beatie, you stay with Abigail, and none of your nonsense. Go on now, off with the pair of you.'

Beatie turned without a word. The two girls climbed up the precipitous Jacob's Ladder.

Abigail thought, 'I'll speak to her on the way home. Tell her the truth, that he may not know he loves Dovey, but he certainly doesn't love me.'

The moment they reached the top of the cliff, Beatie took off like a rocket.

The little girl was fleet-footed, and she had gained strength since Abigail had first known her. She slung her boots around her neck on their laces, and fled down a narrow crevice between two towering warehouses, over a fence and down a series of dog-legged steps. Abigail, surmising that she was taking short-cuts, followed her, her longer steps quickly gaining on Beatie's.

'Beatie!' she yelled. 'You're not to tell Dovey. You don't understand!'

'Shut your face, Judas!' drifted back to Abigail.

Near The Green, she almost caught up with Beatie. Several entertainers were working on The Green: the old beggar with the monkey in the hussar's uniform, playing a tin whistle to which the monkey hopped; a blind singer; and a man playing the bagpipes. The Argyle Cut, just beyond, was crowded with carriages and pedestrians in their Sunday best.

All at once there was a commotion amongst them. Horses reared, men bellowed, a cabbie drove up on the footpath beside the church, sending several ladies with parasols into spasms and screeches.

'Oh, dear God, it's me faither!' gasped Beatie, just as Abby caught up with her. Out of The Cut charged Mr Bow, yelling unintelligibly, sword cutting shining arcs above his head. He made a swipe at the bagpipes; the drones of the pipe, completely severed, flew into the air like so many sticks, and the bag let go its air with a fiendish squeal. The piper, realising that it might have been his bonneted head that had flown in the air, subsided on the grass, uttering hysterical squawks.

A constable waving his staff pursued Mr Bow. As he passed Beatie, he panted, 'He's set the shop afire, wench! Get the Brigade!'

Beatie hovered indecisively, her face yellow with fright. But Abigail picked up her skirts and fled for the shop, and after a moment Beatie followed her. The shop was full of smoke, and Granny was beating at the blazing bench and tables with a wet sack.

A group of urchins, hopping with excitement, clustered about the door.

'Run for the Brigade!' shouted Beatie, 'and it's worth a tanner to you!'

The boys scattered as if by magic, and Abigail and Beatie joined Granny in an effort to smother the flames.

The old woman was exhausted. 'He had drink hid somewhere. He was at it all morning, and then all of a sudden he said, "Here's an end to it!" and tossed the rum bottle into the fireplace. Heaven help me, I thought a cannon had exploded down at the Battery!'

Abigail saw at once that there was no chance of their putting out the fire. A long thread of flame, probably where the rum had splashed, already crawled into the parlour. She said to Granny, 'Where's Dovey?'

151

'Ran upstairs to throw down her bride chest.'

'For the love of Mike!' cried Abigail. 'At a moment like this? Here, Beatie, help Granny out and safely across the street, and I'll go after Dovey.'

'Your gown is in the bride chest, child,' wheezed the old woman. 'That's why Dovey went up yonder.'

Abigail hurdled the first two stairs, which were smouldering, shooting out small bluish tongues of flame. She found Dovey, a handkerchief tied over her nose and mouth against the smoke, trying to drag the chest towards the door.

'Too late,' said Abigail briefly. 'Anything breakable in here?'

Dovey shook her head.

'Out the window with it then. Here, take the other handle!'

They got the chest to the window. Abigail threw the casements wide, and they hoisted the chest out. It slid down the skillion roof and stuck against the chimney-pot. Dovey cried out in horror.

'If it burns, Abby, you'll not get home again, ever!'

'Don't talk,' said Abby. She dipped a towel in the jug on the wash-stand. 'Put this over your head. The stairs have caught.'

Dovey was trembling, but she limped as fast as she could to the door. Now they could hear the crackle of the old dry wood. Abigail snatched the quilt from the bed, tipped the rest of the water over it, and wrapped it about head and shoulders. Dovey stood on the landing.

'I canna do it, Abby, I'm faintish . . . oh, sweet Saviour, where's Granny?'

'She's out and safe. Down you go, Dovey, or I'll push you, I will!' threatened Abigail.

But the girl clung, weeping and coughing, to the bannisters.

'If we go now, we can get clear down the stairs and out of the door,' begged Abigail. 'You must, Dovey, you must, for Judah's sake!'

The stairs were not yet ablaze, but the bannister was warm. Abigail saw that a patch of fire obstructed the bottom of the stairs where the fire had run across into the parlour. It was a rag mat, well alight.

'Here, wrap this round you, and I'll go first!'

She flung the wet quilt over Dovey's head, and taking her hand, got in front of her. Slowly, the lame girl slipping and stumbling, they got around the awkward corner of the stairs.

Now, in full view of the blazing shop, Dovey froze with terror. Abigail grabbed her, hauled her across the smouldering bottom stairs, and kicked the flaming mat aside. She shouted 'Through the kitchen, quick, Dovey!'

'I canna, I canna!'

'You can!' shrieked Abigail, and she pushed the girl through the smoke, down the passage into the kitchen. The little room under the skillion roof was untouched by flame.

Dovey seemed on the verge of collapse, but Abigail shoved her through the back door. 'Get out of the yard, Dovey, in case the roof falls in . . . for God's sake, what are you doing?'

For Dovey, her eyes wild with terror, was struggling to get past her into the hall.

'Gibbie! We forgot Gibbie!'

Abigail had completely forgotten the boy's existence. With blanched faces the two girls stared at each other, then Abigail snatched the quilt from Dovey, and wound the wet towel around her head.

'I'll get him.'

'But Abby . . .'

'Go. Go!' screamed Abigail, 'And right out of the yard,

153

do you hear me? Find Granny and Beatie, so that they know you're safe!'

She thrust Dovey out the back door and closed it so that there would be no added draught. She shut the kitchen door behind her.

The stairs were now alight. Flames curled around the bannisters. The two bottom stairs were a black gaping hole rimmed with jagged rubies. Abigail took a flying leap across them. She sensed the third step give way under her foot, fell forward entangled in the quilt, and felt the tread above her as hot as iron. The smoke was suffocating. She draped the towel over her face and ran blindly the rest of the way. The door to the attic was closed.

'Thank heavens,' she thought. 'It won't be filled with smoke.'

Now she could hear Gibbie screaming. She burst through the door, slammed it behind her, and said tersely, 'No talk, Gibbie. The place is on fire. We'll have to go through the window.'

The little boy had got out of bed and put on his flannel dressing-gown. He was holding his mother's picture in one hand and the framed text 'Thou, God, Seest Me' in the other.

'I wanna go down the stairs like ordinary,' he wailed.

'You do, and you'll be a cinder. *Come on!*'

She tried to open the window, but it had been nailed shut. She picked up the three-legged stool by the bed and knocked out the glass.

Gibbie said, horrified, 'Look what you done!'

She banged out the remaining splinters of glass, looked to see if the child was wearing slippers, and ordered him:

'Come and see for yourself. It's only a little way down to the roof and we're going to get out and scramble down.'

Gibbie approached and looked down with a ghastly face, as though the drop were twenty metres instead of one. He recoiled.

'I'll break my arms and legs and I dinna want that. And I want to do Number One, forbye.'

'Who doesn't?' yelled Abigail. 'The house is burning down, stupid. Do you want to burn, too?'

But he wouldn't move. At last she snatched the picture of his mother from him, dropped it out on the roof, and tearing the text from his grasp, sent it sailing across the room. Then she clouted him once on each side of the head, and while he was opening his mouth to bawl, she grabbed him round the middle, pushed him feet first through the window and onto the roof. Then she squeezed out after him.

'Dinna you think I won't tell Granny, you wicked girl. You'll go to hell, you just see!'

Now that she was outside, Abigail could see that the entire front of the cottage was blazing. A large crowd had gathered, and two leather-hatted constables wielding long staves drove them back towards the shelter of The Cut.

'Listen, Gibbie, the Fire Brigade is coming! Do you hear the horses? And the bell clanging?'

Up from George Street came the fire engine, the horses galloping, men clinging to the sides of the vehicle. A tanker followed behind. Gibbie showed some faint interest, but there was no time for dawdling and staring. Abigail pushed and pulled him down to the edge of the roof. Dovey was nowhere in sight. While Gibbie hesitated and complained and palpitated at the height, Abigail took the opportunity to push the bride chest from behind the chimney-pot and into the next yard. It fell with a clang. There was an outcry of startled Cantonese from the

155

laundry and angry squealing from the tethered pig. She threw the photograph of Amelia Bow into a basket of unwashed shirts.

Abigail tried her best to wheedle the boy to take her hands as she lay on the roof, and swing down to drop into the yard, but he cowered pitiably.

'Gibbie, there isn't time to argue. You just have to climb down. It's hardly any distance to fall, if I hold you.'

'I want to do Number One.'

A Chinese with a pigtail appeared. He chattered helpfully at Abigail, then ran for a large packing crate and put it below the roof.

'I inna going to be caught by any heathen Chinee,' bawled Gibbie. Abigail, with a nod to the laundryman, seized the boy by the armpits and pushed him off the roof. The little man caught him deftly, cooed comfortingly, and lowered him to the ground.

Then Abby swung herself over to dangle from the roof and be helped to the ground by the Chinaman.

Gibbie sobbed, 'I've lost my picture of Mamma, too.'

Abigail retrieved it from the basket and gave it to him. The Chinese, now joined by another, bowed repeatedly. She could think of nothing else to do, so she bowed back, and on this note of courtesy she left by the lane gate and shepherded Gibbie round to Argyle Street.

The firemen, now augmented by several youthful soldiers from Dawes Battery, directed a stream of water onto the fire.

It was not long before they had it under control.

'It's nobbut what you'd call an *enjoyable* blaze,' remarked a voice near by, deprived of a treat on a dull Sabbath.

Still, the shop was gone. Only smoking, malodorous black timbers showed where it had been. The excitement over, the crowd lingered, coughing melodramatically in

156

the bitter smoke, chatting loudly. Mr Bow wasn't to be blamed for the fire, by no manner of means, the way he suffered with the terrible wound he'd had in the battle at Balaclava. Some said he was a hero; he'd been in the charge of the Light Brigade and the Queen herself had sent him a little box of chocolates. They gave three cheers for Trooper Bow as well as the firemen before they dispersed. Fires were common in The Rocks, but it was still a free and exciting spectacle.

Now that it was all over, Abigail's legs wobbled. She felt she had run twenty miles. Her hands were black with smoke and she knew her face was, too. When she spoke, her voice came out as a squeak.

'Look, Gibbie, by the bond store – Granny and Dovey and Beatie. Run to them now and let them see you're safe.'

'Aye, they'll be worried sick!' said Gibbie gladly. He turned to Abigail and said with dignity, 'You hit me, and broke my window and threw away my text and gave me to a Chinaman, and I willna forget to tell my Granny. Aye, and you look out for yourself!'

'Okay. You do that,' said Abigail. She leant against the castle-like wall of the warehouse, feeling that if she took a step her knees would give way.

She saw Judah bound out of The Cut. He ran straight to Dovey and enfolded her in his arms, lifting her off her feet, rubbing his cheek against her smoke-stained one. Abigail could not take her gaze away. His tenderness and anxiety were beyond question. Ah, Abigail knew the melting sweetness in his heart, for it was in her own for him.

He held Dovey close to him, her dishevelled hair under his chin, while he questioned Granny and Beatie. His free arm went out to hold Gibbie, who had hobbled beside

157

him and plainly was indignantly describing his experiences.

It was several minutes before Judah looked around for Abigail.

Abigail turned her face against the sun-warmed stone of the wall.

'Good-bye, Judah, good-bye,' she said.

# Chapter 11

The mighty butcher and his thin, goitrous wife took them in. Abigail was washed, fussed over, acclaimed. The constables brought back Mr Bow, who had relapsed into his melancholy trance-like state.

'I'll not put it down in my notebook this time, Ma'am,' said the senior ponderously to Mrs Tallisker, 'for the sake of the childer, like. But it's got to stop, oh, yes, or there'll be no way of keeping him out of the madhouse. Why, he could have had some poor creature's napper off, snip-snap!'

The butcher retrieved Dovey's bride chest from the Chinese laundry, and brought it to them. He dropped a vast hand on Mr Bow's shoulder as he crouched in the thin wife's tidy parlour.

'Don't fret, Sam, me old cocksparrer,' he assured him. 'I've already put two of me stoutest apprentices in to see none of the villains about here get into what's left of the cottage during the night, and nab your bits and pieces. And as for rebuilding, why, we'll get some of the lads together and have you back in business afore you can say Walker!'

Granny, very wan and shrunken, but somehow tranquil and content, was with Abigail. 'Well, lass, you did what you were sent for. You saved Dovey for Judah, and now the Gift will hae a double chance of survival.'

159

'I think it's immortal after all,' said Abigail. She managed to smile. 'I'd like that. I'm tired,' she added inconsequentially. Her eyes closed in spite of themselves. She knew the mighty butcher gathered her up – for she could smell lamb chops and suet – put her into some bed, but she did not stay awake to find out where she was.

'Stay awhile with us,' begged Dovey the next day, 'for you're one of the family, Abby, true!'

'No,' said Abigail. 'I have to go home; you know that.'

Her green dress looked strange to her; it had been so long since she had seen it. She saw it was not very well made; it was not worthy of the lace-like crochet.

Abigail put on the dress. It fitted more tightly across the chest. My figure's coming at last, she thought. Inside she was cold and without feeling, like a volcano covered with ice.

Granny examined the crochet again.

'Well,' she said gaily, 'I'll hae to live long enough to make it! So maybe I'll be with you all awhile yet!'

Granny agreed that it must be Beatie alone who took Abigail to the corner of the lane in Harrington Street where she had so unexpectedly stepped through the door in the century.

'And with the dark coming down, as it was in your time,' she said.

Abigail began to get anxious that the time would not go fast enough, that whatever numbed her heart would vanish and let the pain free. Especially when she had to say good-bye. Dovey wept as she kissed her.

Abigail thought, 'I ought to be feeling that I could kill her, but I don't.' She said, 'I wish you happiness, Dovey. You deserve it.'

Judah. Could she say good-bye to Judah?

He kissed her cheek, a swift, brotherly dab.

160

'Good-bye,' said Abigail in a low voice. He looked for a moment into her eyes. Did he shake his head, ever so slightly, before he let go her shoulders and hastened away to rejoin his ship? She did not look after him.

'What are ye dilly-dallying for?' cried Beatie tetchily from the door. 'Do you think I want to come home in the pitch dark?'

Gibbie was asleep in bed and Mr Bow did not look up as she said good-bye, but Granny held her close to her corseted bosom.

'Ye think ye've been badly treated, hen,' she said. 'Not so. I told you once and I tell ye again, the link between you and us Talliskers and Bows is nae stronger than the link between us and you.'

'Oh, Granny!' cried Abigail. She gave the old woman a hug. 'I wish you were my Granny in truth!'

'For the love of blanky heaven and all eternity will ye come!' yelled Beatie. The little girl hopped from one bare foot to another. Her face was like a thundercloud.

So Abigail went, hastening down Argyle Street with Beatie, not looking back, for she was afraid to do so.

'There's no reason to be still angry,' said Abigail.

'You shunna kissed him when he was Dovey's,' snapped Beatie. She snorted. 'Any road, how do I ken you won't be back, worming your way 'twixt Judah and Dovey? Because I saw the manner he looked at you when he said good-bye, oh, aye, I saw!'

Abigail suddenly felt weary, tired of Beatie's tantrums, and angry with her, too. She was glad to feel angry, because the anger drove down the sadness.

'I won't be back because as soon as I get home I'll burn the crochet, that's why!'

Beatie slid her a look. 'Honour bright?'

'Take it or leave it!' said Abigail cantankerously.

161

They marched in grumpy silence down the street. It was as crowded as a fairground, for Monday was market day. Outside the Penny Dance Hall hung ornate gas lamps on curly brackets. Though the dark had not come they were lit, their long blue and yellow tongues lolling in the salty breeze.

Abigail saw Maude the dress-lodger outside, surrounded by disarrayed redcoats, already half drunk. The girl was in the most vivid of grass-green dresses; a pork-pie hat full of velvet pansies crowned her fantastic coiffure. The sweet smell of hot gin filled the air.

'Look,' said Abby, pulling at Beatie, 'there's one of the girls from the house in the Suez Canal.'

Beatie pulled her arm away haughtily.

The street was full of stalls and barrows and roped-off enclosures where there were dancing dogs, an Indian juggler, and something mysterious called The Infant Phenomenon.

They turned the corner of Harrington Street, past the Ragged School, where the infants of vanished parents, gutter children who lived in cracks in the rocks and under counters and old doors, were taught the rudiments of civilisation side by side with the children of the respectable poor such as Beatie Bow.

'Beatie,' said Abigail. After a moment she shouted, 'Take that blanky look off your obstinate little mug, will you?'

Beatie unwillingly snorted a laugh, quickly retrieved it, and growled, 'Well, what d'ye want? Spit it out!'

'I want to say that you can hate me or whatever you like, but please go to Mr Taylor and tell him what you already have learnt, tell him that you wish to be educated, girl or not. Ask him if he'll tutor you privately.'

Beatie was startled out of her sulks. ''Twould be

162

improper to approach a gentleman. Faither wouldna permit me!'

'Oh, damn Faither!' cried Abigail. 'You have to look out for yourself, you dummy! How will you ever get anything if you don't march in and bullyrag people into giving it to you? Or maybe you're too chicken-hearted?'

Beatie turned scarlet. She clouted Abigail on the arm with her hard little fist. 'I'll punch ye yeller and green, drat ye!'

Abigail saw ahead of her the lamp that lit the steep stairs to the alley which ran down to the playground. Beatie kicked angrily at the kerbstone. Her face was undecided, back to its crabbed urchin look.

'I know you hate me because I fell in love with your brother. Well, he doesn't love me, never did and never will. And I did save Dovey for him.'

''Twas no more than what you were sent for,' said Beatie churlishly.

Abigail lost her temper. 'Oh, you know everything, don't you? Let me tell you, you sulky little pig, you know nothing about love, that's one thing. You have to experience it to know how powerful it is.'

Here she stopped, dumbstruck, remembering who had said the same words to her.

'Anyway,' she said, 'I lost, didn't I? So good-bye and good luck.'

But Beatie said nothing. She did not even look at Abigail. Abigail left her and went down the stairs. Half-way down the lane she saw the brightly painted loco engine, the space rocket, and the monkey bars, waver out of the twilight, like a superimposed photograph.

She looked back, quickly, saw Beatie growing transparent. The bottle-green shawl turned into a cobweb, the pale little oval of her face shone for a moment and was

163

gone. Did she see an uplifted hand waving her good-bye?

'Beatie!' she cried.

But there was nothing at the alley's top but the worn stairs. The blank walls of tall warehouses made walls for that steep crevice, brightly lit by shadowless electric light from some unseen globe.

Abigail turned away. Her eyes blurred. She saw Mitchell spring into sight, incredibly tall to one now accustomed to little houses scarcely higher than sunflowers. It was a fantastic obelisk, its curved windows reflecting a phantom city of another age.

She gazed at this sight as amazed as Beatie herself might have been – and as she did the last note of the half-hour sounded from the Town Hall clock.

Was it possible? That no time had passed at all? That all the weeks, months, she had lived in another world, the kind of growing-up she could never have experienced in this one, had occurred between one sonorous clang and another?

The thought was so eerie she began to tremble. Time . . . who knew anything about it? Because it passed at the common rate in 1873 was no reason at all to believe that time had also passed in the next century. But it was still winter, as it had been when she left her own time. In the light cotton dress she was chilled to the bone. The brown leaves of the plane-trees, desiccated and fragile as brown paper, skidded past her.

*'But which winter?'*

Nervously she approached the playground. The children seemed to be wearing anoraks and woolly caps that had not changed. Overhead a jetliner arrowed. In its design she could see no change from those she knew.

The lobby of Mitchell beamed with light, but she was afraid to approach it.

'Even if it's next year,' she thought, 'and Mum has gone, what will I do, what will I say?'

But she could not stand there in the freezing wind for ever. Resolutely she approached Mitchell. Something about her feet felt strange. She raised the hem of her skirt and saw that she was still wearing Dovey's circularly striped wool stockings, and Granny Tallisker's best shoes.

'I'll never be able to get them back to her now,' she thought. 'Oh, what will she think of me?'

She ran then into the handsome lobby, into the lift, and upstairs. Suddenly she thought, 'The key of the unit, where is it?' But it was still safety-pinned inside the deep pocket of her dress.

As she unlocked the door she heard what was music to her – Vincent having one of his howling, kicking tantrums next door, and Justine bellowing at him as if she were about to go out of her mind.

'Thank God, thank God,' said Abigail. She switched on the lamps. The clock said twenty to six. A morning paper was tossed on the kitchen bench. Abigail seized it greedily. The date was still the 10th of May. It was incredible. So much had passed, terrors and friendships and shocks, the painful blisses and tender hurts of first love: and it had all happened between one bong from the Town Hall clock and another.

She wanted to fall into the bear chair and cry for days. A burn on her arm stung, her bones ached, the back of her neck was still sunburnt from the cockling expedition. Her heart was beginning to hurt. She would never see Judah again, never in this life or any other.

'I can't think about that,' thought Abigail frantically.

But she knew that after the scene at the shop that day (so far away now she could hardly remember what had been said) her mother would come home early. She ran

165

into her bedroom in panic, ripped off the shoes and stockings and threw them behind the drawer of her divan bed, where all her chief treasures had always been hidden, old diaries and broken beloved toys, and the dress-up clothes of her childhood. A piece of paper fluttered out. On it was written in a childish hand, 'I hope Jann gets pimpels and if I knew a which she would, too.'

Abigail threw it back in amongst the treasures and the dust. How little she had understood anything!

She would think about burning the dress tomorrow. She ripped it off and pulled on sweater and pants. Her face, had it changed? In some indescribable way it had: the skin was paler and finer, and her eyes seemed darker. Or had her eyelashes grown?

'Oh, sugar! My hair!' It had grown nearly to her waist. She shook it out of its plait, still tied with a piece of red ribbon from Dovey's bridal chest, took the scissors and whacked it off to shoulder length. It was crimped horizontally from months of plaiting; her mother would be sure to notice. She knelt down and put her head under the bath faucet, scrubbed her scalp hard.

The front door opened. 'Are you there, Abigail?'

'Sure thing, Mum!'

Quickly she whisked a towel around her wet hair, hid the slashed off hair under her mattress, and went out to the living-room. Kathy was all fluffed-up like an angry bird. Abigail couldn't help smiling like an idiot at her, for she was so pleased to see her, not a day older, not a bit different, just Mum, volatile, loving and her very own.

'What are you grinning at, you little wretch? How could you do such a thing, running away like that without a word?'

'I'm sorry, Mum. It was a childish thing to do. But I was upset and mad with you.'

'Well, that's understandable.' Kathy stopped dead and

stared at her daughter. 'Funny, for a moment I thought you looked quite different. Older or something.'

'It's my sheikh of Araby get-up,' said Abigail, pushing the towel turban rakishly over one eye. But Kathy took her by the shoulders and turned her to the light.

'It's amazing . . . you do look different . . . I suppose I just haven't looked at you properly lately.' She flung her hand-bag in a chair. 'Oh, I've been in a flurry, not thinking straight. You know how I get. No brains to speak of, just fluff.' She stared at Abigail again. 'Just for a moment there I could see what you'd look like in a few years' time. It was sort of – eerie. I forget you're growing up, you see.'

'So do I,' said Abigail. She threw her arms about her mother and almost lifted her off her feet. 'If only you knew how glad I am to see you.'

'Gosh, it was so awful today,' murmured Kathy. 'Imagine us fighting!'

'I did a lot of thinking on the way home,' began Abigail, but Kathy put a finger to her lip. 'Not a word about it. Not tonight, anyway.'

Abigail nodded.

In bed that night Abigail wondered if Beatie had got back home safely.

'But she didn't come into my time. I think Granny was right. Beatie had the Gift just for a little while, during and after the fever. Well, that will please her, little stirrer.'

But most of her thoughts were for Judah. She could not drive him out of her mind. The look in his eyes when he embraced Dovey, all his northern restraint gone, his gratitude and relief.

'Love, you fool, not relief,' said Abigail cruelly to herself. 'He loves her, and why not? She is much nicer than you in every way. But if he could have looked at me that way, just once . . .'

She tried to turn her thoughts in another direction.

167

Tomorrow she would wait till her mother had gone to Magpies, and she would burn the crochet in the downstairs incinerator. Then the door in the century would be closed for ever.

But Judah was so alive, so vivid to her. He filled her mind as he filled her heart.

'I miss him, that's all,' she said.

She knew girls felt like that when they were fourteen or so. She remembered Samantha Peel crying for a solid week when some pop star or other was discovered dead. 'I would have looked after him and made him happy,' Samantha had sobbed, 'even if he was a druggie.' She remembered girls falling crazily in love with teachers and older girls, making pests of themselves with constant ringings-up, and notes, and gifts, and waylayings.

'I'll get over it,' she thought. But she felt she was different from the others.

She'd never had the frequent infatuations of other girls. She'd never been rapt in anyone before. And also there was that knowledge she'd had, that after she fell in love with Judah the empty place inside her was no longer empty. It still wasn't empty, though very soon it would become so.

But now she had to put him out of her head, go to sleep, lead the ordinary life of that ordinary schoolgirl, Abigail Kirk. She jumped out of bed, slid aside the window and leant out into the icy, whipping sea-wind.

'The winds go through you like a bodkin, taking a stitch or two on the way.' She could hear Granny's voice talking about Orkney.

'I have to forget Granny too, and 1873, and Beatie, and Dovey's little ring with the garnet!'

She stared blindly down upon the scintillant city, up at the gemmy Bridge, across at the Opera House, faintly

168

luminous like a marvellous butterfly poised on the sea.

'Whatever did Beatie think of that? A giant's magic palace? I never did have a chance to explain to her.' She gave a sob that was half a snort because of the wind blowing into her mouth. 'That beastly place is more real than this one! And it isn't, it isn't. There probably isn't any shop any more on the corner of Cambridge and Argyle streets. I mustn't cry. My eyes will swell up, and Mum will notice tomorrow morning. I've got to go to sleep!'

She folded up her green dress and took it to bed with her. She stroked it softly, and after a little while she slept.

But her sleep was full of dreams.

They were strange dreams. She saw Trooper Bow, his legs and arms chained together, and the chain threaded through an iron ring on the wall. His eyes wandered wildly, and tears ran down his cheeks in a ceaseless stream. She knew they had put him in the lunatic asylum and his family could not rescue him. She struggled desperately to tell the attendants: 'He's not mad. It's just his wound. He's the kindest of fathers. Don't take him away from the children!'

She saw Beatie in someone's study, for the walls were lined with bookshelves. Beatie sat at a leather-topped table, her head bent over a book. Small and upright, she was not a child any longer, but a young woman. Her hair was plastered smooth and parted with mathematical precision in the centre. The rest was caught up in a black knitted snood or net.

'Oh, Beatie,' cried Abigail gladly, 'what are you reading? Is it Latin? Is Mr Taylor tutoring you after all?'

But Beatie did not hear. Her face was severe and resolute. It was then that Abigail noticed that not only the snood was black; the girl was in mourning.

'But for whom? Not dear Granny? Oh, did Gibbie die after all?'

In a flash the study vanished and Abigail was on a ship. The waves ran along the side, leaping and hissing. They were as grey as marble. The ship rolled and creaked. There was a drumming from up in the air, where the wet sails flickered out showers of salty drops. But she felt no movement. Muffled in his pea-jacket, a woollen cap on his bright head, Judah sat on a roll of canvas, mending some ship's gear, or so she thought. He had not got older as Beatie had.

'Judah!' she cried joyfully, but he did not look up. The pulley and rope in his fingers changed to a knife and a little wooden figure he was whittling. Somehow she knew it was herself. With an exclamation she could not hear, he tossed it overboard, where it turned into Abby herself, clad in Dovey's blouse and serge skirt, rising stiffly up and down in the waves like a statue or a ship's figurehead.

'Oh, Judah,' sobbed Abigail, 'how could you?'

She awoke, confused and frightened, to find her mother shaking her. 'You were having such a nightmare, yelling and crying.' She sat down beside her daughter who was blinking dazedly into the light. 'Are you sure you're all right?'

'He threw me away,' sobbed Abigail. 'But I saved Dovey for him, didn't I?'

'There, there, poor pet,' soothed her mother. 'It's just a nightmare. My goodness, what a dramatic one!'

'Oh, Mum,' sobbed Abigail, 'why is life so awful? Why do people have to put up with so many terrible things? Why is it when you love someone they don't love you?'

'Hush, now,' said Kathy. 'You've been dreaming. It's all right now. You'll have forgotten in the morning.'

Next day Abigail did not speak of her dreams, and her

mother concluded she had forgotten them. But she took her daughter by the shoulders and looked at her searchingly.

'You *are* different!'

'How could I be, Mum?' asked Abigail with a smile. Kathy shook her head.

'Of course you can't be.'

'The main thing is that you're just the same,' said Abigail.

She walked into Magpies with the sensation that she was returning after a long absence.

It was so different from Samuel Bow, Confectioner, so cunningly arranged, so full of vivid or comical treasures. Against the walls stood painted flats from ballet companies which had visited Sydney in Kathy's childhood: Scheherazade's gold-latticed windows and Ali Baba jars; and mysterious avenues of trees from Les Sylphides' enchanted grove. There was an embroidered stool and an autoharp painted with yellow roses, and miniatures of little boys with sailor suits and tomato cheeks.

Kathy was busy cleaning the family pictures she had brought from the sale at St Mary's. Some of the portraits had been hand-tinted.

'Amazing colours the Victorians wore,' she commented. 'Look at this – blue crinoline skirt, magenta jacket, and a yellow feather on the bonnet.'

'The poor people didn't,' corrected Abigail. 'They wore brown holland, and a grey woollen stuff, and a white pinafore. And funny stockings with stripes going round and round like Glasgow Rock.'

'What on earth do you know about Glasgow Rock?' asked her mother.

'Saw it in an old sweet shop window,' replied her daughter truthfully.

She felt defeated and restless, and as Kathy had come almost to the end of her cataloguing and pricing, she asked if she could go home.

Kathy gave her a keen look. 'Feel all right, do you, pet?'

'Bored with holidays, that's all.' Abigail shrugged. 'But I'm not going home to sit in the bear chair and mump. I thought I'd take a walk around The Rocks and look at things. It's such a funny old place.'

Before she went she hugged her mother and said, 'It's all right about Norway, you know.'

'Well, I'm blowed!' said Kathy. She stammered 'But . . . what . . . how . . .'

'I don't know why I made such a fuss,' said Abigail. 'I just don't know. I suppose it was a shock or something. But it's all right. If Dad still wants me to come, too, then I will.'

Kathy's eyes shone. She gave a little jump of excitement.

'Sssssh!' cautioned Abigail. 'A customer. See you tonight, Mum.'

As she hurried up Argyle Street it was almost as if she were going home. She could almost smell the sugary odour of the sweet shop; she looked around to see if Beatie were stamping up the street, frowning and discontented.

But Argyle Street was sunny and deserted. It was not the right time for tourists, or perhaps they were all in the Argyle Art Centre. She went past the Art Centre, and stood under a bare tree and looked at the wall on the corner of Cambridge Street. A brick wall. She didn't know what was behind it, and didn't care either. Across Cambridge Street fluttered strings of laundry just as they had in Granny's time. The traffic bellowed overhead on the highway.

In this sunny, empty world she wandered about; it was

172

clean, and seemingly uninhabited. Was it only last night she saw this street teeming with ragged, grubby, and vital citizens, selling, buying, yelling, exhibiting fighting dogs, piglets, the Infant Phenomenon? The Garrison Church didn't look any different, except that now it had a symbol of the Trinity on its east end. Broken steps that ran nowhere, a tangle of blue periwinkle and brambles, climbed up behind the church to the ridge where the residence of the schoolmaster had stood in what was then Princes Street. Had Beatie ever run joyfully up those steps to Mr Taylor's study, there to achieve the education for which she had been so famished?

It was amazing, terrifying, that all signs of the family's life could have so completely vanished, as if they had never been. It was as if time were a vast black hole which swallowed up all trace of human woes and joys and small hopes and tendernesses. And the same thing would happen to her and her parents.

Abigail turned away, walked through a maze of lanes still familiar. Where the incline became too severe, the alleyway turned into a flight of steps; cottages still clung and perched, or were built into the living rock. The cliffs were water-stained under the winter-flowering vines. Fig-roots snaked down as they had always done. There were still privies at the end of shoebox yards. Only the people had gone, the beggars, the urchins with dirt-stiff hair, the dogs with mange, the hatter with twelve hats, 'all clane'. Queer how independent and jaunty they had been. Poor as dirt, but full of vitality.

She did not dare to go to the top of the cliff above Walsh Bay, where she and Beatie and Judah had climbed down the Jacob's Ladder to the seashore and the dory. It would be all docks, all different.

It was like a dream, and one that hurt as if a knitting

173

needle had been stuck in her chest. The empty place inside her had become so empty she could not bear it any longer and turned towards home. She took her cut-off hair and green dress and went down the back elevator to the big incinerator that belonged to the tower block.

It was easy to rip the Edwardian fabric to pieces. It was perished, anyway, after all. She threw it into the incinerator and poked it down with the iron rake. The crochet yoke remained in one piece. She held it a moment, inhaling those old odours of Dovey's bridal chest, mothballs and lavender and a faint sweetness that came, so Beatie had told her, from the tail of a muskrat, sewn up in muslin.

She threw it in on top of the smouldering rags of her dress. The flames blazed up briefly. She saw a line of crimson run around the outline of a flower, turn black and charred.

'No, I can't!' said Abigail, and she put in her hand and snatched it out. She stamped out the small flames that wagged here and there, shook away the blackened pieces, and folded it up small.

'I didn't say "honour bright" to Beatie,' she remembered.

She put it away with Dovey's stockings and Mrs Tallisker's shoes.

# Chapter 12

A few days later Kathy brought Abigail's father home for dinner. What a good-looking man he is! thought Abigail. As with many people of Scandinavian descent his hair had faded rather than gone grey. From an ashy gold it had turned to ashy silver.

'Oh, Lynnie,' he said, opening his arms.

Her face pressed against his suede coat, Abigail thought of that other time when her nose was tickled by Judah's coarse woollen shirt. Her longing was unbearable. Her father, seeing the tears in her eyes said, 'I feel rather like that myself. And you didn't object to my calling you Lynnie, either.'

Abigail blinked away the tears. What was the use of crying? She was about to enter upon a new life with new people. She wouldn't even have Mitchell or Natalie any more. The world of Beatie Bow would be a whole earth-distance from her in space as well as time.

And surely space would make things better. It was not like time, that could stretch and twist all in a second and turn into some other aspect of itself.

'What a little dope I was, Daddy,' she said. 'But still, I do feel more like Abigail now.'

Kathy Kirk watching, crept silently away to the kitchen. She thought she'd let them get on with catching up.

Weyland Kirk told her of his plans, how they would go

sailing and ski-ing, how marvellous the Norwegian boys were.

'You ought to see them in their blue velvet evening gear,' he said. 'Breath-taking.'

'I can't wait.' She smiled.

'But you're too young for anything serious,' he said.

'I'll be fifteen soon,' she said. He sighed.

'Yes, not so young, I suppose. Old enough for me to explain about Jan? Because I think we ought to have everything clear before we form a family again. Your mother understands but perhaps . . .'

He looked so anxious, so embarrassed, that Abigail smiled.

'You don't have to talk about it, Dad. I know how it was. You thought she was just a kid, and then you found out she was in love with you, and things got complicated.'

'How did you guess –?' He stopped and said painfully, 'Oh, Lynnie – Abigail – I'm so sorry, for everything.'

So it was decided that Abigail would go back to school for a term. It was, anyway, the long summer vacation in Europe during that time, and they would leave for Oslo in August. That would give Kathy time to tie up the ends at Magpies, find a tenant for the unit at Mitchell, and for them all to prepare themselves for a long Norwegian winter.

It was a time when Abigail's long practice at keeping her feelings to herself was useful. She was sure that neither her father nor her mother realised what was going on inside her. And all she knew herself was that the empty place inside her was so desolate that she fancied she could hear winds blowing within it, round and round, looking for some place to rest.

She took Natalie and Vincent to the playground occasionally. The children there had given up Beatie Bow

176

as a game; they were now crazy about something else. Natalie said wistfully, 'It's queer, Abigail, but I never see the little furry girl any more. I wonder where she is?'

'She's probably at home,' said Abigail, 'brushing her hair and hoping it will grow long enough for her to be bridesmaid at a wedding.'

'Who's getting married?'

'Her brother and her cousin.'

Natalie broke into delighted laughter. 'Oh, you're making up a story about her! And did her hair grow long enough?'

'I don't know, Natalie. I'm not really making up a story. And we have to go home, it's getting so dark.'

'All right,' said the little girl docilely. 'But if you think of some more of the story, Abigail, you'll be sure to tell me, won't you? Will she have a new dress for the wedding?'

'I told you I don't know,' said Abigail, so curtly that she was ashamed of herself. For she longed to sit down somewhere with Natalie – some place Vincent would not find them, or any adult – and begin a story: 'Once upon a time, over a hundred years ago, there was a little girl called Beatrice May Bow who had the fever. Her mother died, and her baby brother died, and they cut off all her hair, because that was what they did in those days . . .'

She realised now that not only did she long for Judah, but she was homesick for all the Bows. She wanted to see Dovey kneeling beside her bed, her lame leg stuck out a little askew from that abominable red-flannel dressing-gown, saying her prayers with such simple faith. She wanted to help Granny make skirl i' the pan, which was fried onions thickened with oatmeal and browned, and rather tasty in a disgusting way; or hotch-potch which was just mutton stew; or oatmeal scones to be baked on the heated round of metal called the girdle. She hadn't even finished telling Gibbie the story of *Treasure Island*. She wondered whether anyone ever would, or would he go to his grave without learning the fate of Long John and the parrot.

She had to know what had become of all those people. She had to find out before she left Australia, so that she could still think about them in Norway.

She knew she was doing a stupid thing – like biting on an aching tooth and rubbing salt into wounds, and all the dusty old sayings; but she went to the Public Library newspaper room and asked for the files of the *Sydney Morning Herald* for December 1873, and January and February of 1874. She had to fill in a form stating why she wished to see the papers, and wrote 'Historical Project', which, she supposed, was correct. The enormous bound files were brought and placed on the sloping reading tables. She was amazed to discover that each newspaper had ten or twelve pages of advertisements before the reader came to what she thought must be the major news pages, though there were no banner headlines.

What was she looking for? She knew Judah and Dovey would never dream of putting a notice of their wedding in the newspaper; that was for the grand people of the High Rocks. Just the same, she read down the births, deaths and marriages column. No Talliskers, no Bows.

On the cable page she saw an occasional reference to a name she knew, Mr Gladstone, the Prime Minister of Great Britain, Disraeli, the Duke of Edinburgh marrying a Russian princess. She hadn't known there was another Duke of Edinburgh.

She looked up to see an old man across the table giving her a poisonous look and realised she was turning the stiff old pages with too much of a rustle. Cautiously she turned to the advertisements. Ah, now she was home –

ironmongery departments selling girdles, kerosene lamps, cooking ranges, camp ovens; Mark Foy's corsetry department; David Jones's new shipment of finest velvets, ribbons, osprey and ostrich plumes, ex ship *Oriel*. She was excited, for now she felt that at least the 1870s had really existed, that high-steppers and fashionable ladies bought their hats at David Jones, and when Granny Tallisker's corset wore out she might get a new one at Mark Foy's. Though more likely she'd get a second-hand one from a barrow, she mused, gently turning the pages, the days, the weeks flitting past, throwing up a name here, a headline there, columns of shipping news, random paragraphs, accidental death from bolting horse in Pitt Street, ship *The Brothers* sinks with all hands.

She felt that her heart had stopped. After a little while she realised that her unseeing eyes were fixed on the old man opposite, and he was snarling even more poisonously at her. She returned her gaze to the paragraph. Heavily laden with timber, *The Brothers* had turned turtle in a gale and sunk off the coast a hundred miles north of Sydney. Some of the valuable cargo had drifted ashore and been salvaged. The date was 4 February 1874.

She did not recall walking home along the Quay. As she went into Mitchell's lift, Justine and the two children tumbled out. Justine said cheerfully, 'Bet you're in a fluster, getting ready for Norway. Lucky you.'

'Lucky me,' said Abigail with equal cheerfulness.

It was queer how her legs walked, her arms moved, her hand turned the key in the door. It was just as if her body went on knowing what to do, though her mind was numb with shock. She pulled out the drawer of her divan, took out the crochet, and sat in the bear chair.

'Granny,' she said to the empty room, 'I have to warn him; you know that.'

The crochet was more damaged than she had thought. The heat of the incinerator had made some of the old threads disintegrate. It fell into rags in her hands. She gathered up these rags, held them to her chest, and turned her thoughts with all her might to Granny, Beatie at her bench in the Ragged School – anyone at all who might hear her, help her to get back to some time before Judah embarked on *The Brothers* and drowned.

She felt the force of her love and desperation tighten her whole body.

'*Granny!*' It was a silent yell, as had been the one she had given in her peril at the top of the old warehouse. '*Granny!*'

The living-room began to waver as though it were behind a sheet of gauze that a wind gently rippled. The window that showed sea and sky and the Bridge darkened and was no longer there.

She was somewhere, neither in Mitchell nor back in The Rocks. She was suspended as though in a dream, not hearing or feeling, doing nothing but see. And what she saw was a hackney cab, a knot of white ribbons tied to its door, waiting outside the church, Holy Trinity, the Garrison Church. The lean old horse had a rosette of white on his headband, and the cabby himself had stuck a white rose in the ribbon of his hat.

Abigail gazed at this as though at a picture. She could do nothing, she could only wait. Then Beatie ran out of the church. She was in gala dress, a wreath of yellow and purple pansies on her still-short hair, a white dress with a pleated ruffle. The dress showed white stockings and elastic-sided boots.

Then came Mrs Tallisker on the arm of Mr Bow, both still in their mourning clothes, though Mrs Tallisker carried a small basket of lavender stalks.

'Granny! *Granny!*' shouted Abigail, silently within the silence. The old woman looked uneasily around, then her attention was drawn to the church door, where a crowd of sightseers parted, smiling and clapping.

Judah and Dovey appeared, tall Judah towering above the small lame girl. She wore a plain grey print dress, and a modest bonnet with white ribbons tied under her chin.

'Judah! Don't go on *The Brothers*. She will be lost. Don't, don't!'

But Judah was admonishing a crowd of what were probably his shipmates, skylarking and pushing each other as they came out of the church. Beatie began to throw rice, and immediately the sparrows flew down from the trees on the green and snatched the grains almost under the sightseers' feet.

'Get away, you blanky things!' Abigail could see the words form themselves on the child's lips. Granny smiled and drew the little girl close, saying a word or two to her.

'Beatie, can't you hear me?' sobbed Abigail. 'Oh, Beatie, listen to me, I only want him to live and be happy with Dovey. Don't let him go on that ship!'

But Beatie did not hear. She danced about the bridal pair, kicked at the sparrows, half out of her head with delight.

Abigail was able to look into Judah's face as if she were only a few inches away. She saw his clear ruddy skin, his dark blue eyes, his white teeth as he smiled down at Dovey. He looked through Abigail as though she were made of air.

Some of the bedraggled women in the crowd darted forward to touch Dovey's wedding-ring, as though for luck. Solemnly she held out her hand to them, and Abigail saw the tiny red flash of the garnet in her betrothal ring, beside the thin glint of gold.

Then she and Judah kissed Beatie and Granny and Mr Bow, and Judah lifted Dovey into the hackney. Granny threw the lavender in after them, and stood back, smiling.

'Granny, Granny!' sobbed Abigail. She could see the scene losing its colour, fading like an old painting. Granny looked about searchingly for a moment, as though she had heard something as faint as the cheep of a bird, then turned away and waved her handkerchief after the cab as it slowly rattled away, a crowd of urchins following it and pelting it with old boots.

Abigail felt that her hands were full of dust. She looked down, saw them on her lap. The crochet was nothing any more but two handfuls of crumbled threads. Nothing was left, not a leaf of the grass of Parnassus, not a twist of the rope border. It fell over the bear chair like yellowed frost.

The living-room was very cold. She turned on the electric fire and crouched before it, shuddering uncontrollably.

Somewhere inside her a little thought arose: 'He may not have shipped on *The Brothers.*'

But she did not believe it.

'Good-bye, Judah, good-bye,' she said.

# Chapter 13

When Abigail was almost eighteen, the Kirk family returned to Sydney. They had lived in several countries, and the girl felt an immense gap in both time and space since she had last stepped into the unit on the twentieth floor of Mitchell.

'Quick, look out the window!' squealed Kathy. 'All the new buildings.'

But Abigail was gazing wistfully about her old home.

'Peculiar,' she said to her mother. 'It looks both smaller and larger.'

'And grubbier,' Kathy grumbled, looking at the marks on the walls, the many dents and scratches that were traces of unknown tenants' lives.

'Well,' said Weyland, 'if we can't turn it into something that feels more like home, we'll sell it and find another place.'

'Art deco wallpaper,' mused Kathy, 'fringed lampshades.'

'Red plush toot seats?' said her husband. 'I'll shoot myself.'

Abigail went into the bathroom. It was still the prettiest bathroom she had ever seen, but her face seemed to be at a different level in the vanity mirror.

'Can I have grown,' she wondered, 'as well as all the other changes?'

The face that looked back was not very different from that of the fourteen-year-old who had so often looked into the glass and cursed that she would never be a beauty. But time had thinned the cheeks, taken off a sliver here and put one on there, given the narrow dark eyes long fair lashes that looked engaging against the tanned skin. Norway had lightened her hair, too. It was now a streaky sandstone colour.

'A bit like Beatie's,' she thought. It was queer she could recall Beatie's face better than she could remember her own of four years ago.

It had been a curious four years. They had made those months or weeks or minutes in that other century recede a little, like a dream. For the first year, her memories of her life with the Bow family had seemed bitterly real; she had been torn apart with grief for Judah, a true unselfish mourning that he had not lived to be happy with Dovey, had children, grown old. It had been a long time before she made herself realise that even if he had not drowned, he would have died many years before she herself was born.

'I might have been only a kid, but I did truly love him,' she said, 'and I wanted him to have his life, even though I could never share it.'

Occasionally during those first dislocated miserable months in Bergen she had comforted herself by thinking that she had dreamed the whole story, or created the fantasy because she had been so upset about her parents coming together again. But she knew that was not so.

'And how wrong I was about Mum and Dad, too,' she thought. 'What a silly kid to get so harrowed. And what a sillier one not to realise that adults have as much right to happiness as the young do.'

Her mother peeped into the bathroom.

'What are you mooning about?'

'Just thinking about growing older, looking different,' said Abigail with a smile.

'You look beautiful, I know that,' said Kathy, hugging her.

'You, too,' said Abigail. 'Do you know what, Mother? I think I'll go and see if the Crowns still live next door. Remember little Natalie, and hellish Vincent?'

As she approached the front door of the Crown unit, she almost expected to hear the fearful sounds of domestic battle coming from beyond. But all she heard was a piano. Her heart sank a little. The Crowns had moved, after all. She pressed the bell, and after a little the music ceased and the door was opened by a tall, good-looking boy of ten or eleven. Peering at him, Abigail gasped, 'You can't be Vincent!'

'That's me, all right,' he answered pleasantly. 'But who are you?'

'Abigail Kirk. I used to live next door. I used to take you and Natalie to the playground, remember?'

'Hey, Abigail!' He grinned with genuine pleasure. 'You went away overseas didn't you – Holland or some place?' He turned and called, 'Mum, come here, you'll never guess!'

Justine was overjoyed to see Abigail. The unit had been redecorated and was reasonably tidy. Justine herself looked plump and contented.

'But Natalie, where's she?'

'Oh, she'll be here in a moment, she's out shopping with Robert. It's her eighth birthday, you know. She'll be so thrilled!'

'She won't even recognise me.' Abigail laughed. 'She was so little when I left.'

'I'll get back to my practice, Mum,' said Vincent and,

excusing himself, he went off into the next room. The piano started again.

Justine said excitedly, 'He's so promising, his teacher says – something quite out of the ordinary. Remember what a fiend he was? Well, the moment he started music lessons it acted like magic. He just suddenly became an ordinary, decent kid. Bill and I couldn't believe it. We say prayers of gratitude every night.'

'Bill? Isn't your husband called Robert?'

'No, no; Robert's my younger brother. He's Nat's favourite uncle, being so young. He's only twenty. Should be here soon. Now then, start from the very beginning and tell me about everything. Did you go to Oslo University? Did you have any romances with glamorous Norwegians?'

'Oh, three or four.' Abigail smiled. 'They're irresistible people. Not serious though.'

'You'll die being back in this old mundane place,' said Justine.

'No, not at all. Oh, it seems a bit hot and bright after those northern countries, but I'm going to finish my degree at Sydney University. I'll soon get used to it, and everything that happened in the last four years will seem like a fairy-tale.'

The doorbell rang, and Justine jumped up. An older, bigger Natalie rushed in, her arms laden with parcels.

'And Robert's downstairs with all the big ones,' she cried. Her gaze alighted on the visitor. For a split second she looked dumbfounded; then, yelling 'Abigail!', she dropped all her packages and hurled herself into the older girl's arms. 'Oh, you've turned into a grown-up, but I'd know you anywhere, anywhere!'

As Abigail's arms closed around the wiry strong little body she had an instant pang of regret for the troubled

186

and tearful child Natalie once had been. It was almost as if she were jealous that Natalie had found a braver, surer self without her help. The child's big grey eyes were frank and lively, the mournful little face was gay.

She thought, 'I suppose she's forgotten everything'; but even as the thought entered her mind, Natalie put her lips close to Abigail's and whispered, 'Do you remember the furry little girl?'

Abigail nodded.

'She's always been our secret, hasn't she? Because no one else saw her, you know.'

A key fumbled at the front door, and Natalie shrieked, 'Oh, there's Robert! Wait till you see the super things he's bought for my birthday!'

'How he spoils you monkeys!' scolded Justine as she went to open the door. A tall young man entered, grinning over an armful of large packages. 'Don't jump on me, Natty, or I'll collapse. Where's Vince? There's an un-birthday something here for him.'

Abigail was half-hidden by the arm of a wingchair. She felt as if she were going to faint, as though the blood were draining down to her toenails.

That voice – she felt again the old agony of longing, the tenderness, the unbearable sweetness of being fourteen and drowning in love for someone who thought her a child.

'It's all going to start again,' she thought in panic. 'But it can't; I burnt the crochet. If it does I won't know how to manage it now that I'm older.'

She cringed back into the chair, trying to hide herself until she could collect her thoughts.

'Put all those down and come and meet one of my oldest friends,' she heard Justine say. 'Vincent, stop that racket. Robert's got a surprise for you. Hurry up, Robert.'

She felt him standing there. For a moment she could not look up, she was too afraid.

Justine was chattering. 'Abigail, you must meet my favourite brother, Robert. Robert Bow, Abigail Kirk.'

Abigail raised her eyes.

'It was the most weird thing,' Justine told her long afterwards. 'All you did was to give him the sweetest smile I ever saw. I always thought you a bit of a sobersides, you know – but this! I practically melted. And then Robert said what he said . . . wow, it was really odd!'

'Abby!' the young man exclaimed. Then he turned scarlet and said, 'Oh, I'm sorry. For a moment I thought I knew you. I don't know why I said that; I don't know that people call you Abby for short at all.'

His eyes were deep blue, his hair was fair. He was taller than Judah. His hands were not hard and brown.

'But then, he's lived to be older than Judah ever did,' thought Abigail, 'and he's never worked as hard as Judah.'

The children were making such a commotion over the presents that Justine rocketed away to supervise.

Robert sat down on the floor beside the chair. He shook his head in bewilderment. 'We've never met, have we? You must think me a nut, bursting out that way. Can't think what made me do it.'

All the confused, half-frightened, half-rapturous feelings that had churned in Abigail's interior a few moments previously had gone. Judah had not shipped on *The Brothers*. He had lived, he had lived! The empty place in her heart filled with peaceful benign happiness. She knew that it was settling over her face, that if she looked into a mirror she would see the ghost of a middle-aged woman, still married, still in love, rich with contentment. She almost put out her hand to stroke Robert's cheek as she had dared to do to Judah in that long ago year. But she

188

did not. It was not yet time. He did not know what she knew.

'Tell me,' she said, 'how does your name happen to be Bow when Justine's surname is . . .' she broke off. 'But of course, that's her married name. You must excuse me. I was quite young when I lived in the unit next door.'

'Oh, yes, I know,' said Robert. 'Natalie's often mentioned you. You used to take her to the playground.'

What else, she wondered, had Natalie told him?

'I knew some other Bows once,' she said. 'I had a friend, he was called Judah.'

Robert looked dumbfounded. 'But that's my name too! Robert Judah Bow! Where did you know them? They must be cousins or something. I must ask Justine.'

'No, no,' said Abigail tranquilly. 'She didn't know them. We'll talk about them another time. Just let's sit.'

She wasn't sure afterwards what they talked about. It was too natural and ordinary to remember. She told Robert about Norway, and he told her about the marine engineering course he was doing.

'I've got this feeling about the sea, you see.'

'Yes, of course.'

'I think my ancestors came from Shetland or some-where, so I suppose the sea is in my genes.'

'Orkney,' said Abigail half to herself. He looked at her half puzzled, half fascinated.

'May I come and see you?'

'Yes, of course. I'm right next door.'

They smiled at each other like old friends.

As she went out, Justine whispered, 'Isn't he a doll?'

Abigail smiled. As she bent to kiss Natalie, the little girl whispered in her old way. 'You won't go away, will you, Abigail? Everything's going to come out all right now, isn't it?'

'Yes,' said Abigail.

When she returned to her parents' unit Kathy said, 'We've decided art deco is too frightful. Maybe Norwegian, with the doors painted with garlands and bouquets in dim colours.'

'You'll start a trend,' said Abigail absently. She did not feel she would be living in that unit very long, so she was not very interested in how it would look. Kathy asked her about the Crowns, nodded with pleasure over the miraculous change in Vincent.

'He was jealous of Natalie, you know,' she said.

'Maybe you're right,' said Abigail. 'Kids . . . whoever knows what they're thinking?'

'And who else was there with Justine, that made you look the way you're looking?' asked Kathy, slyly.

'A university student called Robert Bow,' answered Abigail.

'And?'

'He's dropping in Saturday afternoon. You'll like him.'

Kathy was about to say something teasing when Abigail added, 'He's bringing the family Bible.'

Kathy looked bewildered.

'We just want to look up a family tree,' explained Abigail.

At the week-end Robert arrived. He towered even over Weyland Kirk. Abigail saw now that, aside from his height, there were small differences from Judah's in his face. The eyes and hair and features were the same, but the teeth more regular. The smallpox scar that had dimpled Judah's cheek was missing; the hair was cut altogether differently.

'He's had an easier life than Judah, just as I've had an easier life than Dovey or poor little Beatie, probably. I wonder what happened to her?'

The Bible was a mighty volume. The green plush had hardly any pile left at all; the brass edges were black and bent. They had not been polished for many years.

'Justine had it at the top of the linen cupboard. It belonged to some old great-great aunt or such. She used to be headmistress at Fort Street School, you know the old building up near the Observatory that the National Trust has now?'

'So she made it, the little stirrer!' crowed Abigail. She beamed at Robert, who gaped at her.

'She wasn't any little stirrer; she was a perfect old tartar. Mother remembered her quite well; she was in an old ladies' home or something. Mother was petrified with terror of her, she said.'

'Old Miss Bow?' Abigail laughed marvelling. 'Who would have guessed it? I guess that's how that kids' game sprang up . . . terror lest Miss Beatie Bow would rise from the grave and give them all whatfor!' She laughed. 'Sorry, Robert. I must sound like a witch. But after we've looked at your family tree I'll explain a bit.' Her eyes twinkled as she smiled at him. 'The rest I won't tell you until we know each other lots better.'

'That won't be long if I've anything to say about it.'

'Let's go into the kitchen,' she said. 'Those two are fighting over re-decorating the unit. We've been through the red-plush loo seat phase, and I don't want to be present as they pass into the birchwood and Scandinavian, with Lappish rugs. Besides, in there we can put this monster out flat on the table.'

Robert opened the enormous book and turned to one of the thick mended pages. Hand-painted violets and faded ribbons of lilac enclosed the family tree. Each name was in a little painted oval touched with gold paint. Some of it was in a fanciful Victorian hand with long looping tails, the ink bleached to a light brown. Some names were in a round, childish script, and at the bottom the names of Vincent and Natalie Crown were written in Justine's favourite green biro.

Abigail fell upon it eagerly. 'Your great-grandfather, Judah, where's he?'

'Hold on!' said Robert. 'I didn't have a great-grand-father Judah. That's just a family name. My great-grand-father was Samuel, I think.'

'It couldn't be,' protested Abigail. 'That was Trooper Bow's name, their father, Beatie and Gibbie and Judah's father.'

'How on earth –? Never mind now – Gibbie! That was it. Gilbert. Look, here it is.'

His brown forefinger slid down the painted branches of the tree till it landed on *Gilbert Samuel*, b. 1863, d. 1933.

'That's not possible,' cried Abigail. 'He wasn't supposed to live; he wasn't long for this world. What's Gibbie doing hanging around until he was – what is it? – seventy, mind you!'

Robert gazed at her, flabbergasted.

'Then Judah must have drowned after all,' she said slowly. 'Where is he, Robert?'

Her finger went back to the curly Victorian writing. She found *Judah Bow*, b. 1855, d. 1874.

'Oh, Robert, he was on the ship after all. He died at nineteen. It isn't fair!'

'Oh, Judah, oh, Judah,' she sobbed. In a moment Robert had his arms around her. He tried to make sense of her choked mumbles, but all he could get was: 'And when I saw you I was sure he had lived, and Dovey had had a baby, and you were descended from him. How do you look exactly like him then? Beastly little Gibbie! You've no idea how awful he was, always panting to join his mamma amongst the angels. He even had his funeral worked out.' She raised her head and sniffed angrily. 'It's just him to put it all over everyone and live till seventy, little sneak.'

'But if he hadn't lived,' Robert pointed out softly, 'I wouldn't have had him for a great-grandfather, and I wouldn't be here listening to you.'

'I loved him so much,' wept Abigail. 'Not horrible Gibbie, but Judah; and I knew he would be drowned and tried to warn him but I couldn't get back . . . Oh, Robert, he died when he was nineteen, he never had a real life at all.'

'Now then,' said Robert, and there was in his voice the firmness of Judah Bow, who had been a man, with a man's work and authority, at eighteen. 'You're going to calm down and tell me all about this: how you know things about my family I don't know, why you're crying about someone who died more than a century ago. You know you're going to tell me sooner or later, don't you? So why not sooner?'

He kissed away her tears. It seemed a very natural and accustomed thing to do. So, very simply and without embarrassment, Abigail told him what had happened four years before. He listened seriously.

'Natalie has something to do with this, hasn't she?' he pondered. 'Because, after all, she's a Bow, and perhaps she has the Gift. And the crochet, because it came from the fingers of that Great-great-great-grandmother Alice from the Orkneys, was just enough to tip you over into the last century. She was right, you know: you were the Stranger of the Prophecy.'

'But the rest of the Prophecy –' cried Abigail. 'I mean, it was Granny Tallisker herself who believed that one for death and one for barrenness meant Gibbie for death, because he was so frail, and one for barrenness meant

Beatie, because she always said she wouldn't get married no matter what. And instead it was Judah for death, and Dovey for barrenness. The Prophecy was right, but Granny had the wrong people.'

'Dovey wasn't barren,' said Robert gently. 'She's the one called Dorcas, I presume? Look at the family tree again. She had a child, Judith, and it died with her, the same year as she and Granny died.'

'That was the smallpox year,' said Abigail. 'Oh, poor little Dovey, poor little baby. And Granny . . . she was the most wonderful woman. Isn't it strange, Robert, even Granny thought that my importance, as the Stranger I mean, was to go back that day of the fire and save Dovey for Judah, so that their children would have two chances of perpetuating the Gift. But it was getting that little monster Gilbert out of the house as well that mattered. Yes, that was what the whole thing was about. I had to save Gibbie, so that he could continue the Bow family and the Gift.'

She pored over the Bible. 'I suppose there were other children, daughters, perhaps, and some of them had the Gift, too. But whoever has kept the record just hasn't bothered to put them down.'

'I guess old lady Beatie just didn't have time. She was a famous classics scholar and a perfect martinet as head-mistress, so Justine says.'

'The interesting thing is,' said Abigail, 'that you believe all I say.'

'Yes,' he said. 'First of all because it's you telling me, and secondly because it wouldn't occur to me not to. I mean, I had this sensation the moment I met you, that you were so familiar I knew all about you except that it had slipped my mind for a moment. I spent that whole night trying to remember what it was.'

194

'I stayed awake, too,' confessed Abigail. But when he asked her why she would not tell him.

He turned over the page. 'There's lots more room for the family to go on,' he said, 'and already painted. Funny, these flowers are wattle and Christmas bells. They must have been done after the Bows and Talliskers arrived here as immigrants.'

Abigail thought that perhaps Dovey had painted those flowers because entwined amongst them were sprigs of lavender, bog cotton and grass of Parnassus. Poor home-sick Dovey, a wife for such a short while, a widow for only two years.

'You would have liked Granny Tallisker,' said Abigail. She sighed. 'You won't care for mine; she's even worse than she used to be.'

She was silent, thinking of that old woman, Alice Tallisker, her infinite goodness and strength, and how she had said that the link between Abigail and the Talliskers and Bows was no stronger than the link between that family and Abigail. The theory she had had when wandering The Rocks four years before – that time was a great black vortex down which everything disappeared – no longer made sense to her. She saw now that it was a great river, always moving, always changing, but with the same water flowing between its banks from source to sea.

How on earth had ugly, tempestuous little Beatie managed to get as far as being headmistress of Fort Street High, the foremost school of its time?

'I'll find out how, some day,' thought Abigail. 'Maybe I helped a little, but I'll tell Robert about that some other day.'

Her mother came into the kitchen. 'What on earth are you kids doing?'

195

'Just fooling around,' said Robert. He was still shy with Kathy and Weyland. 'Nothing much.'

'Just playing Beatie Bow,' said Abigail. She knew her mother did not understand, but that didn't matter. Robert did.

F
PAR          Park, Ruth

             Playing beatie
             bow

DATE DUE                    26333

| BRODART | 06/80 13.95 | | |
|---------|-------------|---|---|
|         |             |   |   |
|         |             |   |   |
|         |             |   |   |
|         |             |   |   |
|         |             |   |   |
|         |             |   |   |
|         |             |   |   |
|         |             |   |   |
|         |             |   |   |
|         |             |   |   |